MACAHAN'S LAW

When a lonely way station is attacked by the notorious Colbert gang, the marshal stops a bullet in the fight. Young Ezra Macahan finds himself with a heavy responsibility. The marshal's dying words: 'Take the Colbert brothers into Santa Rosa and turn 'em over to the sheriff.' It's a tall order, and Ezra will have to fight every step of the way to get it done. The final showdown sees Macahan go from boy to man . . . and from man to lawman.

STEVE HAYES

MACAHAN'S LAW

Complete and Unabridged

LINFORD
Leicester

First published in Great Britain in 2015 by
Robert Hale Limited
London

First Linford Edition
published 2018
by arrangement with
Robert Hale
an imprint of The Crowood Press
Wiltshire

A catalogue record for this book is available
from the British Library.

ISBN 978–1–4448–3660–8

Published by
F. A. Thorpe (Publishing)
Anstey, Leicestershire

Set by Words & Graphics Ltd.
Anstey, Leicestershire
Printed and bound in Great Britain by
T. J. International Ltd., Padstow, Cornwall

This book is printed on acid-free paper

This is for you, Jilly

'All this happened almost twenty years ago.
But I can still remember it like it was yesterday.'

Marshal Ezra Macahan

1

I didn't know how far I had walked since I'd shot my horse.

But I did know the sun had been low on the horizon when I started out and that it was now directly overhead, so I knew I'd walked at least a dozen miles.

In the relentless, broiling New Mexico heat it felt more like fifty.

The horse, a chestnut mare that I'd won in a poker game in Deming, had been unruly and I guessed that she'd only recently been broken. But despite no saddle and with just a rope halter, I managed to stay on her back and headed for the Mexican border.

I never made it.

After only a mile or so the skittish mare accidentally stepped in a prairie dog hole and fell to her knees, throwing me off. I landed hard, my head bouncing off a rock. Stunned, I lay on the hot sand for a few moments, waiting for my head to clear. By the time it did and I could focus, the mare had regained her feet and was standing in front of me, trembling and holding up her left foreleg.

One look told me that her leg was broken. It hung at an unnatural angle and flopped around every time she made the slightest move.

Damn, I thought. *If I didn't have bad luck, I wouldn't have no luck at all.*

I watched the mare flailing around for a moment. I was low on cartridges and hated to waste one on a horse; especially a horse that would end up dead anyway. I'm sure that sounds callous, but cartridges are damned expensive and I had only a few dollars to my name.

Oh, I know that most folks — especially easterners — like to think that a 'cowboy's best friend is his horse'. But that's storybook hogwash. Ask any wrangler who has handled a *remuda* during a cattle drive or broken broom-tails for a living, and he'll tell you that horses are necessary but *definitely* not their best friends.

Even so, I hated to see the mare suffer. So, drawing my Peacemaker, I pressed the gun against her head. 'Sorry, gal. Reckon your luck ain't no better than mine.'

The mare stared at me. I may have imagined it or maybe was just trying to ease my conscience, but I swear she looked grateful. I thumbed the hammer back and fired. The gunshot echoed in the vast, sun-scorched scrubland and the mare collapsed with a thump.

Making sure she was dead, I holstered my Colt .45, removed my battered US Cavalry officer's hat and wiped the sweat from my face. I felt like I was melting. I looked around. The horizon was empty in all directions. Expelling my frustration in a long weary sigh, I jammed my hat back on and trudged toward the border.

Now, hours later and with the sun

scorching my back, I labored up a low barren hill. My legs felt leaden and it seemed to take forever. When I reached the top, I paused to catch my breath and was surprised to see a stagecoach relay station not more than a half-mile away. Coming from Texas, I wasn't familiar with New Mexico and hadn't known there was a stagecoach line so close to the border.

It was a welcome sight. I hadn't eaten since noon yesterday and my first thought at seeing the cluster of low buildings and corrals was to wonder how I could scrounge a free meal — or, as a last resort offer to do a few chores for one.

Hopefully, I thought as I plodded down the sunbaked slope, it wouldn't come to that. As long as I could remember, work never agreed with me. I disliked it as much as responsibility. And since I had no glowing plans for the future and wasn't driven by ambition to reach lofty goals, I'd spent the last few years drifting from town to town, doing odd jobs and charming everyone with my dimpled grin and homespun politeness in order to get what little money I needed to scrape by.

As I approached the relay station, a woman with silver-streaked black hair and a sour, pockmarked face emerged from the barn and crossed to a single level adobe house bearing a sign: Cactus Wells Station.

I couldn't tell her age. She looked about fifty. But she was so spry I figured she was younger and that eking out an existence in the raw, sunbaked desert had prematurely aged her. Yet by her determined, tight-lipped expression I sensed she had enough grit to endure any kind of hardship life threw at her — and would never whine or be bitter about the hand she'd been dealt.

In that respect she reminded me of my mother, whom I hadn't seen in years. She was tall like Ma, too, only much leaner; gaunt in fact. She wore a long blue cotton dress that countless scrubbings and the relentless sun had bleached almost white, a man's straw hat with a frayed brim, and scuffed, high-top button up black shoes. There were bits of straw clinging to the front of her dress, suggesting she'd been kneeling, and the basket on her arm was filled with eggs as brown as her lined, weathered face.

She stopped in mid-stride as she saw me standing by the corrals. She stared hard at me, as if trying to decide if I was real or if she was hallucinating, and then called out to someone in the house.

Within moments a tall, big-shouldered boy cradling an old side-by-side shotgun came hobbling out on a crutch. He was a good-looking kid, with unusually pale almost white-blue eyes, unruly dark hair and his mother's sad expression. His swollen right ankle was bandaged and each step made him wince. He paused on the porch, asking: 'What is it, Ma?'

His mother hooked a thumb my way.

The boy steadied himself against the door and leveled the shotgun at me. 'Who are you, mister? What do you want?'

'Just some w-water,' I said hoarsely. 'Had to shoot my pony a-ways back an' I been walkin' in this God awful heat ever since. Got me a powerful thirst.'

'You a horse soldier?'

I shook my head.

'Then where'd you get that hat?'

'Took it off a dead Apache.'

'You kill him?' the woman asked.

'He give me no choice.'

'Happens.'

I shrugged, but didn't feel any need to say anything.

The woman gave me a final scrutinizing look then said: 'Come inside, mister. It's all right, Gabe,' she added when her son didn't move. 'Let him pass.'

Grudgingly, the boy lowered the shotgun, wedged the crutch under his arm and hobbled back into the house.

I turned to the woman and removed

7

my old sweat-stained hat. 'Much obliged, ma'am.' I politely let her enter ahead of me.

2

There were no windows in the three-room house, just rifle slits in the whitewashed adobe walls indicating the builder had feared attacks by marauding Apaches or, worse, Comancheros. As a result the only fresh air came in through the open door and with little or no breeze today, the inside was stifling hot and smelled of cooking.

A long table with two bench seats occupied the center of the main room.

Dishes, silverware, a loaf of home-baked bread, mugs and a pitcher of water had been set out on the table, with enough places for eight people.

The woman carried the basket to the kitchen area. 'There's water in front of you,' she told me. 'Help yourself.'

'Thank you, ma'am.' I poured myself a glass and drank greedily. The water cooled my parched throat and instantly refreshed me. I refilled the glass, drank half of it then leaned back in the chair and watched as the woman put a big iron coffee pot on the hot stove. She then went to the sink and started cracking the eggs into a bowl. At the same time, she told her son to keep an eye out for the stage.

'What about him?' Gabe said, meaning me.

'He'll be fine. Now go on, boy, do like I say.'

Giving me a warning look, Gabe turned and limped outside.

'Your son's a mite unfriendly,' I told the woman.

She shrugged. 'Being a man means bein' responsible.'

'That another way of sayin' don't pay him no mind?'

She chewed on that for a moment, then picked up a wooden fork and began whipping the eggs. 'Ever since his pa died, Gabe's been obliged to be the man of the house and it's a role he's taken to heart.'

10

'Reckon I know how that feels.'

'You lost your pa?'

I nodded.

'Yet you still left home?'

I nodded again.

'Didn't you feel no need to look after your ma or family?'

I shrugged indifferently and avoided her inquisitive gaze.

'You're right,' she agreed. 'It ain't none of my business, mister.' She turned back to the stove and went on whipping the eggs.

I felt bad. She'd invited me into her home and given me water and here I was being rude.

'I'm not tryin' to hide nothin', ma'am. It's just . . . not long after Pa died Ma got hitched again and the man she took up with, Mr Stottlemeyer, made it plain as gravy he didn't want me around.'

'And your ma, she didn't object?'

'She had no choice. My two brothers and sister needed a father and Mr Stottlemeyer, he was a mighty eligible widower. He didn't take to the bottle too much, or lay a strap on us too often, and read aloud from the Good Book which made Ma happy. He also had this fine house on the edge of town an' owned the general store, which meant he could put food on the table far better than most.'

'I see . . . ' The woman paused and wiped her weathered face on her apron. 'So you lit out?'

I nodded.

'That must have hurt.'

'Some.'

'I meant, for your ma.'

'Reckon. I hear tell she cried a lot.'

The woman grunted. 'Yeah, well, we mothers get plenty of practice doin' that. What might be your name?'

'Macahan, ma'am. Ezra Macahan.'

'From Texas?'

'Yes'm. Brazos.'

'Thought I recognized the twang in your voice.'

I sensed she wasn't finished, so I kept silent.

'How long you been driftin'?'

'Since about your son's age.'

'Fifteen? That's quite a spell.' She gave me an appraising look before adding: 'You must be what — a few summers past twenty?'

'Thereabouts.'

'Mean you ain't sure?'

I shifted my feet uncomfortably, causing the plank floor to creak. 'Ma . . . she got typhoid soon after I was born. It made her awful sick for a while and affected her memory some. But from what she and others remember, twenty-six or seven is close enough.'

'I'm sure it is . . . ' The woman unconsciously touched her pock-scarred cheek before continuing. 'I'm Mrs Elizabeth Moonlight, though most folks 'round these parts call me Beth.'

She seemed to enjoy talking, so I let her talk.

'I'm from K.C. originally. My daddy, he was president of the Mercantile Bank there and, well, he and momma, they wanted me to marry this young fella they had picked out for me. But by then I'd already met Seth — that's my late husband, Seth Moonlight — and I knew right away that he was the one for me. So when he asked me to run off with him, I — ' She paused, catching herself, then laughed self-consciously. 'Will you listen to me? Chatterin' away like a lonely jaybird. And you a total stranger . . . ' She went back to whipping the bowl of eggs and was silent for several minutes. When she was finished, she put a lump of lard into a black-iron skillet on the stove, waited for it to melt then poured in the eggs. 'I'm guessin' you're hungry as well as thirsty, Mr Macahan?'

I nodded.

'Food won't be nothin' fancy, mind, but they'll be plenty of it.'

I smiled my thanks and finished my water.

'Ain't much of a talker, are you?'

'When need be.'

She chewed on that before saying: 'Tell you what: the stage is due here any minute now. It's my responsibility to not only feed the passengers, but to hitch up a fresh team. Gabriel normally handles that — '

'Gabriel?'

'That's my son's name. But he hates it, so we all call him Gabe for short. Anyway,' she continued, 'as you can see, he's limping badly on that sprained ankle. So if you'll take over for him, after the stage leaves I'll feed you the finest meal this side of Lordsburg. That sound fair, Mr Macahan?'

I thought of how tired I was and how much effort it was going to take to change a six-up in the broiling heat and was about to say no. Then my stomach growled, reminding me how hungry I was, and I nodded grudgingly.

'I'll take that as a yes,' Mrs Moonlight said, adding wryly, 'You know, you remind me of Seth. He wasn't one to waste words, either.'

I didn't know how to answer that, so I kept quiet.

'Ever harnessed a six-up?'

I shook my head.

'It ain't hard. I've done it myself, when Seth was — well, in his cups. Trick is to keep the horses calm and the traces from gettin' tangled.'

'I'll manage.'

'Sure you will.' She stirred the scrambled eggs with a wooden spoon before continuing. 'Fresh horses are in the corral by the barn. I'll have Gabe go with you 'case they start acting up. The boy has a natural way with them, like his pa — '

She stopped as Gabe stuck his head in the door. 'Ma, stage is comin'!'

'Yes, I can hear it, Son.' She brushed a strand of sweaty gray hair back from her face. 'Mr Macahan, here, is goin' to change teams for us. You go with him an' help all you can, y'hear?'

'Aw, Ma, I don't need nobody to — '

'Darn it, boy, quit your jawin' and do like I say! *Pronto*!'

Reluctantly, Gabe turned and limped toward the nearest corral.

I gulped down another glass of water

and hurried out after him.

Mrs Moonlight sighed wearily, picked up a kitchen knife and began slicing thick rashers of bacon from a slab of pork belly.

3

The bacon was already sizzling in the skillet by the time the westbound Barlow-Sanderson stagecoach arrived in a swirl of eye-stinging, throat-choking dust.

Leaning against the corral fence I watched as the dirt-caked Concorde coach approached the station-house. As it got close the old, long-haired, white-bearded driver, Capp Riggins, pulled back on the lines, slowing the lathered horses. At the same time he stamped on the brake, causing the wheels to lock up and skid on the dry red earth.

'Cactus Wells, folks!' he shouted. 'We'll be here thirty minutes. Food an' hot coffee's a-waitin'. Everybody out!' Wrapping the lines around the brake handle, he slapped the dust from his clothes and turned to the guard riding shotgun beside him. 'Give the marshal a hand, Rusty.'

'Sure thing, Capp.' Rusty Yaris, a burly man whose sunburned face was almost hidden by a full red beard and a Stetson pulled over his eyes, spat the dust from his mouth and climbed down before any of the passengers got out.

Once on the ground, he faced the nearside door of the stagecoach and stood there, shotgun cocked, watching as four of the passengers got out on the other side. The other three remained seated.

One of them, a small, wiry man of sixty in a black suit, black hat and black string-tie looked out the window and nodded curtly at the guard. He had a drooping gray mustache, sun-squinted gray eyes and a thin-lipped mouth that seldom smiled.

'Easy on them triggers, Rusty,' he said grimly. 'I want these boys to choke on a rope, not die from that scattergun.'

'Don't worry, Marshal. 'Less'n they make a run for it, I don't aim to cheat

19

the hangman. My only regret is I won't be in Deming to watch 'em dance.'

The two big, hard-faced men seated across from Marshal Tom Cady glared at Rusty. Though they were disheveled and unshaven I recognized them from the wanted posters I'd seen pinned up in various Texas and New Mexico jails I'd spent the night in — the Colbert brothers!

Close to my age, they and their older brother, Judd, were part of a gang wanted throughout the Southwest for murder, bank-robbery and rustling. They'd eluded lawmen and bounty hunters for over three years and by catching these two Marshal Cady could retire knowing he'd cemented his place in frontier lore.

The four passengers had reached the station-house. The marshal waited for them to go inside then opened the coach door and wagged one of his two long-barreled Colt .44s at the outlaws. 'OK, climb down. An' remember, boys, go slow. No sudden moves.'

Sloane Colbert pulled himself to his feet, wrist-and leg-irons clanking, and stepped down from the coach. Rusty kept the scattergun trained on him. Behind Sloane, his younger brother Laird also got up but defiantly stood in the doorway for a moment.

The marshal prodded him with his shooter. 'You heard me. Move it.'

Laird, with taunting slowness, got out of the coach. Then raising his manacled wrists, he pointed his finger like a gun at the slim, dark-haired, neatly-dressed passenger who'd paused in the doorway of the station-house.

'Bang!' he said, and grinned as the young woman flinched.

Rusty, seeing her fearful reaction, angrily jabbed the barrel of his shotgun into Laird's belly, doubling the outlaw over.

'That's enough!' barked Marshal Cady.

'Sonofabitch deserved it — and more besides.'

'Don't matter,' the marshal said,

stepping down. 'I'll not tolerate any rough stuff. Now kindly step back and let 'em pass.'

Rusty obeyed, but kept his shotgun trained on both outlaws as he and the lawman escorted them to the station-house. On the way three fluffy baby chicks scurried across their path. Laird kicked one, sending it flying. It landed several feet away, fluttered briefly and then lay still. I heard Rusty curse Laird, who laughed and spat a stream of snuff-juice on the dead chick.

I knew it was only a baby chicken that eventually would have ended up in a cook-pot anyway, but just the same I couldn't help feeling bad for it.

As the outlaws reached the door of the station-house, Marshal Cady called out to everyone inside: 'We're comin' in, folks. All of you . . . keep your distance!'

I watched the three men disappear inside and then finished harnessing the six fresh horses. Gabe insisted on checking everything I did. Though it galled me, I shrugged it off. I mean what the hell? I knew I'd be on my way in another hour, so what was the point of causing a fuss and maybe missing out on a fine meal?

'Satisfied?' I said, as he stepped back.

He nodded reluctantly. I could tell he was disappointed that I'd harnessed the team correctly. I smirked, just to rub it in, and led the horses to the stagecoach. Gabe hobbled after me, moving as fast as his crutch would allow. He then held the team while I unhitched the lathered horses and turned them loose in the corral.

'Hang the tack in the barn, mister.'

I obeyed and then left the corral.

'Double check the gate, mister. Make sure it's closed.'

It was more than I could take. 'Goddammit, boy, quit yappin' at me. I been around horses all my life!'

'Maybe so,' Gabe said, fixing me with his pale-blue eyes. 'But you ain't been around Ma.'

'Meaning?'

'She hears you cussin' like that an' she'll send you a-packing without feedin' you.'

I had no comeback.

4

The fresh horses were full of oats and high-spirited and I had trouble hitching them to the stagecoach. Gabe watched me sourly for a few minutes then finally pitched in. His experience and soothing voice helped gentle the team and when the job was finished, I felt obliged to thank him.

Oddly enough that didn't sit well with him. He stared at me suspiciously. 'You won't get no extra meal by toadying up to me, mister. Ma gets to say who eats and how much 'round here.'

'I ain't lookin' for an extra meal, sonny. Soon as my belly's full I'm headed for the border.'

'Why? You got some flea-bit Mex' whore waiting in Chihuahua?'

I grabbed him by the shirt-front and jerked him close. 'My belly might be empty, boy, but if it comes down to eatin' or pounding some manners into you, I'm willing to miss another meal.'

Gabe pulled away, steadied himself on his crutch and glared at me. I could tell he wanted to curse me. But he must have seen the angry glint in my pebble-gray eyes, warning him not to press his luck, and he bit back his words.

I also must have earned his respect, because when he next spoke he'd lost his belligerence. 'You best go eat, mister. Ma only fixes so much food an' them passengers look hungry enough to chew the fur off a dead coyote.'

'What about the horses?'

'I'll handle 'em.'

'Fair enough.' I started for the house.

'Them prisoners,' Gabe called after me, 'what d'you figure they done?'

I looked back at him. 'You name it, they done it.'

'Yeah,' Gabe agreed. 'That's what I figured.' He stared enviously at the heat-wavering horizon before adding:

'Ever been to Lordsburg?'

I shook my head.

'Me neither. Pa kept promisin' to take me there, but then he caught the pox an' died . . . ' His voice trailed off and he again stared at the horizon.

He looked so glum I felt sorry for him. 'I lost my pa when I was about your age,' I said.

'Yeah? How?'

'Rustlers. He caught 'em runnin' off some beef. He drew down on them but one came up behind him and — '

'Shot him in the back?'

I nodded.

'So he was a cattleman?'

'Lawman. Yours?'

'He wasn't much of anything — 'cept a drunk who stole Ma's money to buy whiskey. But he was still my pa and I loved him plenty.'

Empathizing with him, I said: 'Want me to bring you some grub when I'm done eatin'?'

'Uh-uh. I'll eat leftovers with Ma after the stage leaves, like always.'

All the fire had gone out of him. He looked as lonely as I sometimes felt.

'Sorry about your pa, Gabe.'

'Thanks.' He hunched his bony shoulders. 'Like Ma says: we'll survive.'

It was the same thing my mother had told me. I'd believed her, because she had never lied to me. But it hadn't made me feel any better than the boy did now.

'Sure you will,' I said encouragingly. Feeling his pain I tousled his unruly hair for a moment then turned and entered the station-house.

5

Earlier I hadn't paid much attention to the other four passengers; I'd been more interested in the Colbert brothers. But now, as I sat at the table and tucked into the bread, scrambled eggs, bacon and bowl of ham hock stew that Mrs Moonlight had served me, I saw that three of them were men in their thirties, while the third was the woman who'd flinched when Laird Colbert pretended to shoot her.

The men were interesting. Two of them wore custom tan Stetsons, western suits, string ties and hand-tooled cowboy boots and I pegged them for wealthy cattlemen. The third man was dressed in range clothes, had shoulder-length tawny brown hair and the tanned, lean face and sun-strained eyes of a desert rider. He seemed ordinary enough until I noticed the gun holstered on his hip. It was a nickel-plated Smith & Wesson Schofield revolver with fancy bone grips and the cut-away holster was tied down, gunfighter-style. That wasn't all. Every movement he made was unhurried and deliberate and the way he kept glancing about him, as if expecting danger, made me wonder if he was on the run.

As for the woman, I wasn't sure about her — but, then, I'm ain't sure about any woman. No matter how hard I try, I can never figure them out. Just when I think I know what they're going to do next, they do something else. What's worse, when you call 'em on it, they shoot you this uppity look and you end up feeling like the problem is your fault. It frustrates the hell out of me. Which is why I don't have much dealings with women — 'cepting whores, of course, which, being a necessity, don't really count.

This woman wasn't more than twenty-five or six. She was dressed primly enough to be a school-teacher, yet she was too tanned to have spent her life in a classroom. She also wore lip rouge and perfume behind her ears that smelled like violets after a rain — which I found puzzling for someone who taught schooling. She was prettier than any teacher I'd ever seen, too, and there was a swing to her hips that any dancehall girl would have envied.

I've never been around a true lady, though folks in Brazos say Ma was close to it, but I've heard tell they're polite and mostly shy. That's why I was surprised when this woman noticed me staring at her and instead of blushing or looking away, as I'd expected, continued to look brazenly at me with eyes I'll never forget. Green as moss agates, they seemed to gaze right into my soul. It was like just by looking at me she could tell what type of person I was and it made me feel damned uncomfortable.

'It's rude to stare, you know,' she said, her voice low and husky.

The other passengers stopped eating long enough to give me dirty looks. I didn't give a hoot what they thought of me but for reasons I couldn't explain, I wanted the woman to like me.

'A gentleman would apologize,' she chided.

I felt my cheeks burn. 'Wasn't my intention to be rude, ma'am. It's just that you . . . ' I didn't finish, knowing my excuse would sound lame, and went on eating.

The woman, whose long, loose dark hair touched the table when she leaned forward to eat, wouldn't let me off the hook.

'I — what?' she demanded. 'Remind you of someone?'

I nodded.

She smiled, eyes sparkling, so damned pretty it made my heart jump. 'Who would that be, Soldier — your sweetheart?'

'I ain't a soldier. And I don't have a sweetheart.'

'Who, then?'

'My sister, Ellie. Only you're much older.'

'*Older?*' She made it sound like an insult. 'Well, all I can say is I hope Ellie's your kid sister.'

Everyone at the table laughed. Everyone but Marshal Cady, that is. One look at his cold, flinty eyes told me that nothing made him laugh — 'cept maybe a good hanging.

'She is, ma'am. Fact is she's the youngest of us all.'

'And the prettiest, I'll wager?'

I nodded — even though it wasn't true.

'Then I'm obliged to forgive you,' the woman said, and the way she said it again made everyone but the marshal laugh. She then offered me a slender gloved hand, adding: 'I'm Sarah Eckers.'

'Ezra Macahan,' I said, shaking hands. 'It's a pleasure, ma'am.'

'Miss,' she corrected. 'I've yet to tie the knot.' She smiled, held my gaze for another moment then continued eating.

Laird, who according to the wanted posters was the youngest of the three

Colbert brothers, wiped his mouth on his sleeve, making his wrist-irons clank, and grinned at me. 'What're you waitin' for, mister? Quit lollygaggin' over your food an' act like a man: take this whore out back an' hump her till your head hurts.'

Everyone at the table was so shocked they stopped eating. As one, they looked at Sarah, at me, and then back at Sarah.

Steamed, I jumped up and jerked my Colt.

'Damn you,' I hissed at Laird. 'Apologize to the lady.'

'What lady?'

'I said — apologize!'

'Like hell.'

'If you don't, you won't live long enough to get back on that stage.'

Across the table from me Marshal Cady, who hadn't moved, said softly: 'Leather your iron, mister.'

'Not 'fore he apologizes.'

'I said, leather it!'

'I'll swear I'll shoot him if he don't.'

'You shoot him and I'll see you hang for murder, 'longside his brother.'

I hesitated. I could tell he meant it, but now that I'd drawn my gun I couldn't see how I could holster it without losing face.

Laird, seeming to understand my predicament, gave me a needling grin. 'Looks like you've bitten off a sight more'n you can chew, fella.'

No one at the table moved; most of them didn't even breathe.

'Please, Mr Macahan,' Sarah begged, 'do as the marshal says.'

'See?' Laird said mockingly. 'Even the whore don't want you to hang.'

'Shut your damn' face!'

Laird laughed. 'You got lots to learn about women, mister. Hell, just 'cause she's not dressed like a whore don't mean she ain't one. Tell him, honey,' he said to Sarah. 'Tell him how Sheriff Whitehill run you out of Silver City for chiseling quit claim deeds from all of them miners you bedded upstairs in the White House Saloon.'

Sarah gave him a wintry stare, but maintained her composure. 'I'm afraid you're mistaking me for someone else, mister. I've never been to Silver City.'

'The hell you ain't!'

Before Sarah could argue, there was a shot outside and a bullet whined in through the half-open door and punched a hole in a big, ornate wall-mirror. Shattered glass flew everywhere.

6

Startled, everyone hit the floor.

Several more shots followed, some of the bullets breaking the remaining glass while others came in through the door and ricocheted off the walls.

'You in the house,' yelled a man's voice. 'This is Judd Colbert. Me'n my boys got the place surrounded. Let my brothers go or we'll kill all of you!'

Marshal Cady, who was crouched at one of the three window slits, motioned for everyone to stay down and then yelled: 'No deal!'

'I'm warnin' you, Marshal,' Judd replied, 'either you let Laird and Sloane walk out of there or I swear to God, we'll gun you all down.'

'Marshal, maybe we ought to do like they say?' said the older cattleman.

The marshal didn't answer him; didn't even bother to look at him. To the outlaws, he shouted: 'If you know who I am, mister, then you must know my reputation for never makin' deals with renegades. So you'n your men either ride on out of here or make your play. Call it.'

There was a moment of silence then all the outlaws opened fire.

A hail of bullets peppered the walls, shattering dishes, knick-knacks and pictures and ricocheting around the room.

Everyone flinched.

The marshal looked at the two cattlemen and hissed: 'Get to the windows and start shootin'. And try to make each shot count. You women,' he added to Sarah and Mrs Moonlight, 'I need you to reload. Oh, and if you got any extra guns or ammo, Mrs Moonlight, fetch 'em.'

She nodded and turned to her son, saying: 'Bring me my Henry, boy. And then get your scattergun.'

As Gabe obeyed her, she kicked the door shut then slid open a rifle slit in the upper section. 'Not to argue with you, Marshal, but seeing how many of 'em there are, you'd be better off lettin' me shoot while the young lady does the reloading.'

Marshal Cady nodded in agreement and continued shooting through the slit before him.

I moved alongside him, asking: 'Where do you want me, Marshal?'

He looked around, then said: 'Since there ain't enough windows for all of us, you keep an eye on those two misfits.' He thumbed at Laird and Sloane, who were hunkered down by the rear wall. 'An' if they so much as hiccup, shoot 'em.'

'My boy can do that,' put in Mrs Moonlight. 'Mr Macahan, here, if he's willing, can maybe turn the tide before that trash out there decides to burn us out.'

'I'm listenin',' Marshal Cady said.

Mrs Moonlight pointed at the floor under the table. 'See that handle stickin' up? It's a trap-door. It leads down to a tunnel. My husband dug it out in case we were ever attacked by Apaches or Comancheros.'

'Where's it come out at, ma'am?'

'Beyond the rocks those devils are shootin' behind.' She moved back from the door slit so I could peer out.

The rocks were twenty paces away and I could see men crouched behind them, firing at us.

'Now the tunnel ain't been used in a spell,' she went on, 'so it might be caved in. But if it ain't and you can make it all the way, you'd come out behind that trash. That way you can get the drop on them an' maybe drive 'em off.'

The marshal nodded thoughtfully. 'What do you think, Mr Macahan?'

'They won't go quietly.'

'Reckon not.' He studied me, sizing me up before adding: 'You ever killed anyone, young fella?'

I was about to lie and say yes, but his flinty gaze told me that he'd know if I was lying.

'No. But don't be sweatin' over that.

Pa took me huntin' soon as I could walk.'

'Killin' animals ain't the same as killin' a man.'

'Maybe not. But I know one thing,' I said, as the outlaws' bullets punched holes in the door, 'I won't lose no sleep over shootin' these bastards.'

'Good man. But remember, caution's the way. You get careless an' take a bullet, we're done for. They'll burn us out, then gun us down an' leave our corpses for the buzzards — save for the women. For them, it'll be worse.'

I wasted no time picturing what would happen to Sarah and Mrs Moonlight. Hurrying to the table, I pushed it aside, grabbed the iron ring and pulled up the trap-door. It was stuck and it took all my strength to raise it. A moldy stench flooded up from the cellar, making me gag. Someone joined me with a lighted hurricane lamp. I saw it was Mrs Moonlight.

'Here, you'll need this,' she said,

handing me the lamp.

'Thanks.'

'The tunnel gets a mite narrow near the end. But you can still squeeze through. My husband did an' Seth was bigger than you.'

'Don't worry, ma'am. I'll make it.'

''Course you will. Good luck.'

I pushed my hat back off my head and started to lower myself into the tunnel. As I did I glanced at Sarah, who was deftly reloading the cattlemen's pistols. She smiled at me. It was the kind of reassuring smile that made me feel special — you know, like she trusted me to save everyone. And as I dropped into the dank-smelling cellar I promised myself that I wouldn't fail her.

7

The tunnel hadn't caved in but cobwebs and tangled tree roots blocked my way. I used my knife to hack through the roots and brush the cobwebs aside and, lamp in one hand, crawled slowly along on my elbows and knees. The dank moldy stench almost choked me and my head still throbbed from when the horse had thrown me, but I thought about the way Sarah smiled at me, which helped shut everything else out of my mind and kept me moving as fast as I could.

The tunnel wasn't too deep and I could dimly hear shooting going on above me. I could also hear my heart pounding. I kept telling myself to hurry. It wasn't easy. Like Mrs Moonlight had said, the tunnel got narrower near the end and squeezing through it slowed me down. I tried to widen it by stabbing at the walls. But big chunks broke off, causing the dirt overhead to shower down on me. It got in my eyes, half-blinding me, so I quit. What was even more frustrating, when I wiped my eyes with my knuckles it made them water, so I quit that too.

I inched my way along and finally reached the end. I held up the lamp and by the flickering flame saw a trap-door above me. Made out of nailed planks, it wasn't as wide as my shoulders and was white with cobwebs. I tried to cut through them with my knife, but they stuck to the blade and, worse, spiders rushed to repair their webs.

I jerked my hand back before any of them reached me. Damn spiders! I hate 'em. Always have.

Then an idea hit me. Removing the glass chimney I held the flame to the cobwebs. They burned with a faint crackling hiss. Singed, the spiders fled. I replaced the chimney and saw a piece of board jutting out from the earth near my shoulder. Guessing that Mr Moonlight had put it there as a shelf, I set the lamp on it then used both hands to raise the trap-door. It wouldn't move. Knowing it probably had either a lot of dirt or rocks on top of it I hunched down on my knees, pressed my back against the door and pushed upward.

It took all my strength but slowly the door began to rise. I could hear gunfire nearby, much louder now, and hoped that none of the Colbert gang was looking my way. By their constant shooting I guessed they weren't. They were probably too focused on keeping the marshal and the others pinned down in the station-house to worry about being attacked from behind.

I cautiously raised the door high enough to see out. I was right. The outlaws were crouched down behind the rocks, their backs to me. I blew out the lamp and, gently, so as not to make any noise, wriggled out from under the raised door.

It took a few minutes but finally I

was out in the open. I quietly lowered the door behind me. I lay there, motionless, for a few moments to make sure none of the outlaws had seen me. Then, satisfied they hadn't, I crawled behind some nearby bushes and drew my Colt.

I knew what I was supposed to do. I aimed at the nearest outlaw, a short scrawny man firing a Winchester, and tried to pull the trigger. I couldn't. Shooting a man in the back, even an outlaw, went against even my cynical principles.

But I had to do something. And fast. Grabbing a stone I hurled it at the same outlaw. It bounced off his leg. He whirled around to see who'd thrown it — saw me and started to shoot.

I fired first. My aim was true and he slumped down by the rocks. Startled, the outlaw next to him turned toward me. I shot him too. The bullet hit him in the chest and he dropped his rifle and collapsed. Several of the other outlaws now looked in my direction. I quickly fired at them, missing one and winging another. Then I ducked down behind the bushes and quickly reloaded.

I heard an outlaw shouting that they were being attacked from behind. The others — I'd counted nine or ten — began firing at me. Ricocheting bullets shredded the bushes above my head. I ducked lower and finished reloading. My heart was racing and I felt more alive at that moment than ever before. What's more, I was surprised to realize that killing someone hadn't made me feel as bad as I'd expected.

After a little there was a lull in the shooting. Taking advantage of it, I crawled behind a nearby rock, peered over the top and fired at the outlaws.

One of them yelped and clutched his arm. The other dived for cover. I ducked down, expecting all of them to fire at me. Before they could, a barrage of shots poured out of the way station.

I looked over the rock and saw Marshal Cady, the desert rider and the two cattlemen firing out of the now-open door of the house. The outlaws fired back.

I waited a few moments. They seemed to have forgotten me and I quickly shot two of them. The others, realizing they were caught in a cross-fire, lost interest in a shootout and sprinted for their nearby horses.

I emptied my gun at them. But I shot too fast and didn't hit anyone. And before I could reload, they swung up into their saddles and spurred away.

I stood up, heart pounding, and ran to the men I'd shot. All were dead. I know it's a terrible thing to kill a man and for an instant I felt badly. Then I reminded myself that they were out-laws, ruthless killers who'd robbed and burned and raped and suddenly I felt pretty damned proud of myself. Hell, if I hadn't risked my neck in that tunnel, who knows how the shootout would have ended?

I'm not one to brag, but I hoped that Sarah would appreciate what I'd done and from now on save all her smiles for me.

As I walked toward the station-house I noticed that the cattlemen and the desert rider were hunkered down beside Marshal Cady. The old lawman sat slumped over on the ground and as I got closer I saw he was clutching his belly. Blood reddened his fingers. I realized he'd been gut-shot and was fading fast.

'He wants to talk to you,' the desert rider told me.

He spoke so softly I barely heard him. ''Bout what?'

Instead of answering, he stepped aside allowing me to kneel beside the marshal. Blood came from the lawman's slack mouth and his eyes were glazed.

His lips moved with great effort. I bent close and put my ear to his mouth.

He kept mumbling, his words so jumbled I had to listen to him several times before I understood what he was saying. It wasn't something I wanted to hear. I started to tell him that I couldn't do what he wanted, but he suddenly gripped my wrist and stared at me, eyes blazing, and as if gathering his last drop of strength, said: 'Promise me, Soldier.'

'I ain't a soldier.'

'Your word . . . Give me your word on it.'

I hesitated.

'Your word, mister. Your word!'

I didn't want to give him my word. Truth is it was the last thing in the world I wanted to do. But the desperation in his bloodshot eyes dragged it out of me.

'All right,' I heard myself say. 'You got my word.'

Instantly, I regretted it. Once I give my word I keep it and that meant I'd have to delay my trip to Mexico. I started to tell him that I'd changed my mind — but before I could, he died.

Cursing myself, I gently closed his eyelids and lowered him to the ground.

'What'd he say?' the younger cattle-man asked as I stood up. 'Sounded like he was askin' you something.'

'Me and my partner couldn't make sense of it,' the other cattleman said.

Realizing that I was the only one who knew what Marshal Cady had said, I was about to lie and say that I couldn't understand him either. Then my conscience chewed on me, like it does occasionally, and before I could stop myself, blurted: 'He wanted me to do somethin' for him.'

'What?'

I hesitated.

'You can tell us, son,' said the older cattleman.

'He . . . told me to . . . take the Colbert brothers on into Santa Rosa and turn 'em over to the sheriff there.'

The cattlemen swapped looks, their expressions saying that I'd be a damned fool if I did.

'But you ain't a lawman,' the desert rider said softly.

I didn't answer.

'Don't reckon you're even a soldier.'

'Never claimed to be.'

'Then why'd the marshal choose you?' asked the young cattleman.

I shrugged, wondering the same thing.

'What're you aimin' to do?'

I shrugged again.

'You surely ain't goin' to do like he asked?'

I started to say no — then noticed Sarah watching me from the doorway of the house. She was smiling, just like earlier, and not wanting to disappoint her or make her think I was a coward, I said: 'Dunno. I ain't decided yet.'

'I'd think long an' hard on it, if I was you, mister,' the older cattleman said.

'Yeah,' his partner agreed. 'Mighty long an' hard.'

'That's because you're not the man he is,' Sarah said, approaching. She stopped before me, cupped her gloved hands about my face and smiled. It was a smile full of promises . . . made all the more irresistible by the fragrance of wet violets. 'If you were, gentlemen,' she continued, looking at me but talking to

52

the cattlemen, 'you'd honor the request of a dying lawman.'

Hearing Sarah talk about me like that filled me with a pride I'd never felt before. Now some folks might say I was getting a swelled head. And maybe they'd be right. But then again, maybe they wouldn't be so quick to judge me if they had met Sarah . . . or smelled her perfumed hair . . . or she'd smiled at them the way she was smiling at me now.

'Miss Eckers is right,' I said. 'If that's what Marshal Cady wanted, then by God that's what I'm goin' to do.'

The desert rider stepped close and spoke softly to me.

'Say again,' I said.

He raised his voice just enough to be heard. 'If it's all right with you, *amigo*, I'll ride along with you.'

'I welcome it,' I said. I then tipped my hat to Sarah. 'If you'll excuse me, ma'am, I better go round up the Colberts and tell the driver I'll be taking 'em on into Santa Rosa.'

'I'll come with you,' she said, slipping her arm through mine. 'It's not often I get to be with a man as honorable as you, Mr Macahan.'

'Please,' I said, 'call me Ezra.'

8

We buried Marshal Cady behind the barn.

There was no time to build a box, so we wrapped his body in one of Mrs Moonlight's old horse blankets. I forced the Colbert brothers at gunpoint to do the digging, figuring that it was only fitting since it was their gang who'd killed the lawman. They cursed me and swore that my days were numbered. But their threats didn't bother me because I'd never expected to die in a rocking chair anyway.

Afterward, Mrs Moonlight kindly read a few passages from her Bible over the dead lawman. Then I had the Colberts fill in the grave and cover it with rocks so the scavengers couldn't dig up the corpse. They obeyed me in angry silence. I kept them covered while they worked, knowing they'd jump me if I turned my back on them. But they didn't try anything, and as soon as they were finished I slung the marshal's gunbelt over my shoulder and escorted the outlaws to the stagecoach.

It was now late afternoon, but still oven-hot. The desert rider stood off to one side, smoking. The other passengers were gathered on the shady side of the coach. By their scowls, I knew they weren't happy about my taking the Colbert brothers to Santa Rosa. The two cattlemen made it clear that they expected the rest of the gang to attack us between here and Santa Rosa, and didn't believe we could fight them off.

'What're you suggestin',' I said, bristling, 'that I turn these bastards loose?'

'Goddamn right,' said the younger cattleman. 'It's the only chance we got of savin' our necks.'

'How you figure that?'

''Cause then the gang's got no reason to attack us,' his partner said. Turning to the sullen-faced outlaws, he added: 'Tell him. Go on. Tell him that if we let you go your men won't come after us.'

'That's the sweet Gospel truth,' Sloane said. He smirked at his brother and held his manacled wrists out to me. 'Do like he says, mister. Unlock these irons an' give us a couple of horses. I swear you'll never see us again.'

For a moment I was tempted. Then I remembered my promise to Marshal Cady.

'Quit yappin' and get in the coach,' I said. 'You too,' I told Laird. 'And remember, if you and your brother cause any trouble, I'll gut-shoot you an' leave you for the coyotes.'

'You damn fool,' he hissed. 'You'll never make it to Santa — ' He broke off, alarmed by something he saw over my shoulder.

I turned and looked in the same direction and what I saw chilled my blood. Spiraling up from the nearby hills were puffs of smoke. I knew instantly that they were smoke signals

— just as I knew that the answering flashes of light winking from the opposite hillside were made by a mirror held toward the sun.

'Apaches!' I said, pointing. Then as everyone looked at the smoke signals: 'Quick! All of you — get in the coach!'

Alarmed, the passengers fought each other to scramble inside.

The desert rider, who'd been studying the smoke signals, joined me and said quietly: 'It ain't Apaches, *amigo*.'

'How do you know?'

'I can read smoke.'

'Who, then?'

'Comancheros.'

The word chilled me. Comancheros were ruthless border trash who rode with renegade Comanches. Killers themselves, before each raid they fed the Indians liquor and goaded them into a vicious, blood-thirsty frenzy.

'Keep a lid on it,' I said, looking at Sarah and the other passengers. 'Reckon everyone's plenty scared enough as it is.'

The desert rider nodded. 'If it's OK with you, I'll ride up top. It's mighty crowded inside.'

'Good idea,' I said. 'And if it comes to it, don't be afraid to use that rifle.'

I thought he might not like me giving him orders. But he just grinned. 'Don't worry, *amigo*. When it comes to savin' my skin, I ain't afraid of nothin'.'

'Glad to hear it.' I stuck out my hand and told him my name.

'I'm Luke Cassidy,' he said, shaking hands.

My mouth dropped.

'Reckon you've heard of me?'

'Who ain't?'

'Yeah . . . ' He sighed, resigned. 'Well, just 'cause you hear things don't always mean they're true.'

'Don't mean they're lies, neither.'

'True. And I ain't tryin' to sugarcoat all the gun-fights I've been in. Or all the men I've killed. But I've never drawn first an' just once it'd be nice if folks didn't condemn me 'fore they knew me or the circumstances — maybe even gave me the benefit of the doubt.' Before I could reply, he bent down, scooped up a handful of small stones, dropped them in his pocket and climbed onto the box beside Riggins.

It was strange. A few hours ago I'd been free of responsibility and just happily drifting. Now, I was responsible for not only making sure two outlaws were turned over to the sheriff in Santa Rosa, but for the lives of everyone on the stagecoach as well. What was even stranger, it felt almost natural.

I started to get into the coach then paused as I saw Mrs Moonlight and Gabe standing, watching us from the station-house.

'What're you waitin' for, ma'am?' I yelled. 'Quick! Get in the coach.'

'No,' she said. 'This is our home. We're not goin' to be driven off by a bunch of renegade — '

I cut her off. 'Think of Gabe,' I barked. 'You want to see him staked out over an ant hill?'

The thought alarmed her. Grudgingly, she pushed her son toward me, saying: 'Do as he says, boy. Go on. Hurry!'

'What about you, Ma?'

''Be right along.' She ran into the station-house.

I helped Gabe climb into the overcrowded coach. He sat squeezed between Sarah and the cattlemen. Across from them sat the two outlaws. I kept my gun on them, pulse racing as I waited for Mrs Moonlight.

Shortly, she came running up carrying a carpetbag and her Henry repeating rifle. I helped her into the coach where she sat by the window next to the outlaws.

'Get goin'!' I yelled at Riggins and swung up into the coach. Inside there wasn't any room on the seats, so I sat on the floor, back to the door and kept my gun trained on the outlaws.

Riggins cracked his whip and yelled at the horses. Startled, they plunged ahead, pulling the coach after them.

Seated on the box beside him, Luke Cassidy started throwing stones at the horses forcing them to run even faster.

We raced across the open scrubland. The sandy trail was full of ruts and in places had been washed away by flash floods. But it was the only trail there was and the fast-moving coach followed it, bumping along, jarring everyone.

I turned and looked out the window at the hills. The smoke signals had stopped but, even as I looked, some twenty mounted Comancheros appeared along the ridge. The leader, a fierce-looking, dark-bearded man wearing a black high-crowned sombrero and riding a white stallion, signaled to his men to follow him and spurred his horse down the hillside.

I turned to the Colbert brothers. ''Fore this day's over,' I said, 'you two may wish the marshal had lived long enough to take you to Deming.'

9

Neither of the brothers responded and at first glance they seemed untroubled. But their narrowed eyes betrayed them. They were full of fear and I knew they were as worried about the Comancheros as the rest of us. As if to confirm it, Laird looked out the window at our pursuers and uneasily licked his lips.

'Take these off,' he said, holding out his manacled wrists, 'an' give us our guns back.'

I almost laughed. 'I must look dumber than I think.'

'Goddammit, we got a right to defend ourselves.'

''Mean the same *right* you gave Charley Boxmeier . . . or Matt Nillson . . . or the Handley brothers?'

'They were armed, same as us,' Sloane protested.

'Yeah, an' they weren't shackled,

neither,' snarled Laird.

'But they *did* have their backs to you,' I reminded. ''case you've forgotten and are claimin' they died in a fair fight.'

'Whoever told you that is a God damned liar,' exclaimed Laird. 'Me'n my brothers, we never back-shot none of them sonsofbitches.'

'Nor anyone else for that matter,' put in Sloane.

'That a fact?' I said. 'Then how come that Texas Ranger in Laredo and those two bank guards in El Paso you killed all had holes in their backs?' I said no more. There was no more to say. I knew they were lying and they knew that I knew.

Just then gunshots rang out behind us.

I looked out the window. Through the rooster-tail of dust swirling up from the wheels I could just make out the Comancheros. They were roughly a hundred yards behind us and gaining fast. The riders in front were shooting at us with rifles.

Up top I could hear the driver cracking his whip and yelling at the team to go faster. But the horses were already at a dead run, making the stagecoach sway dangerously, and I knew it was only a matter of time before it overturned or our pursuers caught up with us.

I pulled my head back in and turned to the cattlemen. 'If you fellas ain't eager to see your bones bleached white by the sun, then get ready to swap lead 'cause we're about to have company.'

They quickly drew their Colts, spinning the cylinders on their forearms to make sure the six-guns were fully loaded.

'I can shoot,' Sarah said, holding her hand out to me. 'Give me one of the marshal's pistols.'

I hesitated, afraid that she might get hurt. Then, knowing her fate would be worse if the Comancheros caught us, I gave her one of the long-barreled Colt .44s.

'I can shoot, too,' Gabe told me. 'Give me the other one.'

He pointed at the marshal's remaining six-shooter, tucked in the holster lying between my feet.

I looked at Mrs Moonlight. She met my gaze without fear. But in her dark eyes was the look of a mother begging me not to let any harm come to her son. Then she looked away and grimly poked her rifle out the window.

'I got a better idea,' I said, drawing my Colt and the marshal's. 'I'll do the shootin', and you reload for me? How's that sound?'

'Fine,' Gabe said. 'Y'hear that, Ma? I'm goin' to reload.'

'That's fine, Son.' She looked at me and smiled gratefully.

I turned back to the window to see how close the Comancheros were.

My blood chilled as I saw they were closing fast. They were now fanned out and all of them were firing at us. Bullets zipped past me, wood splintering as they struck the coach. I pulled my head back in and saw that the passengers were looking at me, as if awaiting orders.

'Start shootin',' I barked. 'And make every damn shot count.' I didn't bother to see if they'd obeyed me but stuck my gun out the window and began firing at the Comancheros.

I emptied the gun but due to the swaying and jolting of the coach, I hit only one man who was riding next to the leader. The bullet punched him from his saddle. He hit the ground, rolled over and was immediately trampled by the horses of the other Comancheros.

I gave my gun to Gabe to reload and started firing the marshal's .44. I had better luck with it, and saw two more Comancheros fall from their horses.

As I again swapped guns with Gabe, I saw Sarah and the cattlemen were firing out their windows. Kneeled between them Mrs Moonlight was trying to pick off Comancheros with her Henry. But the jolting ride was affecting her aim too, and she, like everyone else, was getting frustrated.

'Aim for their horses,' I shouted. 'They make bigger targets!'

'I ain't shootin' no damn horses,' growled the young cattleman.

'Then you're a fool,' Sarah told him. She took careful aim at the leader's white horse and fired. The bullet caught the horse in the chest. It stumbled and fell to its knees, throwing the leader off its back.

Impressed by Sarah's accuracy, I fired at one of the other horses and it too went down, spilling its rider.

Incensed, all the other Comancheros blazed away at us.

Everyone in the coach quickly pulled their heads back in; simultaneously, up top I heard the driver yelp then start cursing. I guessed he'd been hit and wondered how badly. Moments later the coach slowed up and I knew he must have dropped the lines. Hoping that Luke would grab them and take over the driving, I peered out the window and saw that our pursuers had almost caught us.

Laird Colbert must have guessed the same thing, because he thrust his wrists out to me and again urged me to unlock the irons.

'I can't,' I said.

'If you don't set us free,' Sloane warned, 'we're all goin' to die.'

'It ain't that I don't want to,' I said. 'I don't have the keys.'

'Then shoot 'em off,' growled Laird.

'Even if I did, what good would it do? I don't have any extra shooters.'

'Ours are in the marshal's bag on top. Now, shoot these sonsofbitches off me so I can climb up and get 'em.'

I saw Sarah looking at me. She nodded, indicating I should do as Laird said.

Trusting her, I told him to hold his hands out the window and shot the chain linking the wrist-irons. It shattered, freeing his hands. I did the same to his ankle-irons, setting him free.

Opening the door, he gripped the

roof and pulled himself up on top of the coach. It had picked up speed again and I could hear Luke yelling at the horses.

Sloane, meanwhile, was holding his wrists out the window. 'C'mon! Hurry! Shoot,' he shouted at me.

I fired, setting his hands free. Moments later, Laird's head and shoulders appeared upside down in the doorway as he hung from the top of the coach.

'Here, give this to my brother,' he said, offering me a gunbelt containing two Colt .45s. I grabbed it and Laird disappeared.

I started to give the gunbelt to Sloane then hesitated, for a moment filled with misgivings. But as bullets from the Comancheros — now riding alongside the coach — punched holes in the interior, I realized I had no choice and gave the gunbelt to the outlaw.

He drew both shooters and immediately started firing at the Comancheros, knocking two of them from their saddles.

Knowing I'd made the right decision, I leaned out my window and blasted away.

Our combined withering fire not only killed several Comancheros, but warned the others that we weren't easy pickings. Before long, they wheeled their horses around and rode back to their leader, who was removing his saddle from the dead horse. He yelled angrily at them. I couldn't hear what he said, but by their reactions I knew he'd shamed them. One of them quickly grabbed the saddle while another helped his leader swing up behind him, and they rode back to the hills.

Luke reined up the horses and the coach slowed to a halt.

Grateful, I pulled my head back in. Everyone was laughing, shaking hands and congratulating each other. Their relief was contagious and briefly I got caught up in it. Then I realized the outlaws were still armed. Aiming my

Colt at Sloane, I ordered him to hand over his irons.

He hesitated and I sensed he was contemplating making a break for it.

'Don't try it,' the young cattleman warned him. He trained his gun on the outlaw and Sloane reluctantly lowered his shooters.

'Take off your belt,' I said, taking his guns back. When he obeyed, I tied the belt around his wrists and told the cattlemen to keep an eye on him. I then jumped out of the coach and pointed my gun at Laird.

'Get down,' I ordered.

Luke, who was seated on the box beside the wounded driver, levered a round into his Winchester and also covered the outlaw.

'Best do as he says,' he whispered to Laird. 'Been enough blood spilled today.'

Laird grudgingly tossed his Colts on the ground beside me. 'Just remember this,' he said grimly, 'without me'n my brother cuttin' down a bunch of them

Comancheros, you wouldn't be alive now.'

I knew he was right. 'Tell you what,' I said. 'When I hand you two over to the sheriff, I'll tell him how you helped save our necks. Fair enough?'

'Reckon.'

'OK. Now climb on down, so we can get movin'.'

10

It was dusk when we finally reached Santa Rosa. Originally a small dusty pueblo inhabited by Mexicans, outlaws and border trash, now, thanks to the railroad and a ruthless, powerful cattleman named Stillman J. Stadtlander, it was a thriving cow town with a respectable hotel, a bank, boardwalks, cantinas and false-fronted stores lining both sides of the main street.

Until a few years ago the only law was the US marshal and his deputies who were headquartered in El Paso. Then, from the gossip I'd heard in various cantinas, Stadtlander insisted that the citizens elect a sheriff. As inducement he paid to have an office and a jail built and then promptly bribed enough voters to get the 'pawn' he'd chosen elected.

Now as the stagecoach bumped

across the railroad tracks, past the crowded cattle pens and on up the main street I started looking for the sheriff's office.

It was near the Hotel Carlisle, across the street from a cantina, and I yelled up to Luke to stop the stagecoach in front of it. He obeyed, and then jumped down from the box. Standing by my door, rifle ready, he made sure the Colbert brothers didn't cause me any problems and at the same time that none of their gang showed up and tried to help them escape.

Thanking him, I escorted Laird and Sloane to the office. The door was open and just before entering I glanced back and saw Sarah being helped down from the coach by the younger cattleman. She smiled at me and pointed first at herself then at the hotel, indicating that this was where she was staying. I nodded to show I understood then told the outlaws to keep moving.

Inside the sheriff's office a creaking ceiling fan fought a losing battle with the heat. It merely swirled the hot air around, forcing the flies to settle on the window facing the street. They buzzed and kept flying against the glass, sounding like tiny hammers.

I glanced around and realized this was no different than any other sheriff's office I'd been in, except maybe messier, and prodding the outlaws ahead of me I stopped in front of the desk.

A large, fleshy man in soiled, rumpled clothes sat sleeping with his boots up on the desk. The boots were badly scuffed and had holes in the soles. But in sharp contrast to his soiled appearance, his pearl-gray Stetson was immaculate. It could not have looked newer if it had just been taken out of its box. The wide spotless brim was pulled down over his eyes, hiding most of his face, but below it I could see his graying gunfighter's mustache and noticed he needed a shave. I also noticed a sheriff's star on his food-stained brown vest and that his big gnarled hands were clasped across his ample belly.

He wasn't what easterners pictured a sheriff should look like, but I'm not quick to judge; besides, I wanted to ditch my responsibilities as fast as possible. I moved to the desk and cleared my throat loud enough to be heard over his snoring.

He didn't hear me, so I kicked the desk. Startled, he stopped snoring, made a garbled choking sound as if he'd swallowed his spit, then pushed the brim of his immaculate gray hat up and stared at me with bloodshot eyes. For a moment he was too sleepy to grasp the situation. Then he saw the remains of the wrist-irons and ankle-irons on the outlaws, abruptly swung his boots off the desk and sat up.

'Who the hell are you?' he demanded, as if trying to cover up the fact that I'd caught him sleeping.

I told him.

He chewed on the name for a beat before saying: 'Never heard of you, an' I know all the lawmen in this territory.'

'I ain't a lawman, Sheriff. And 'fore you ask me, I ain't a soldier either.'

'Then what the hell you doin' with these prisoners?'

'Keeping a promise.' I saw that he didn't understand, so briefly described what had happened. 'They're the Colbert brothers, Laird and Sloane,' I added.

'I know who they are,' the sheriff said. Rising, he came around his desk and confronted me. I'm six feet but he towered over me and had me by at least fifty pounds. 'Where's Marshal Cady now?'

When I explained, he looked shocked.

'Cady's . . . *dead?*'

'We didn't shoot him,' Laird said as the sheriff glared at the outlaws. 'My brother an' — '

'Shut up,' the sheriff snapped. Then to me: 'You his kin?'

'Nope. I just happened to be at Cactus Wells when the gang jumped us. Look,' I added, before he could throw any more questions at me, 'I'm on my way to Mexico, so I'd be obliged if you take these men off my hands and let me make some dust.'

The sheriff eyed me shrewdly. 'What about the reward?'

'Didn't know there was one.'

'Well, there is.'

'Glad to hear that.'

'Legally, you ain't entitled to it, you know.'

'Never said I was.'

He thought for a moment, a faintly guilty look narrowing his sun-strained eyes. 'Tell you what, son: I'm a fair man, and when we get to Deming, out of the goodness of my heart, I'll see you get a slice of it.'

'I ain't goin' to Deming, Sheriff. Like I told you, I'm headed for the border.'

'Not if you want any of that reward.'

I wanted it but I wanted to get to Chihuahua more.

'You keep it.'

'Suit yourself, son.'

'Could use a horse, though.'

The sheriff took a bent nail from his

pocket and picked his teeth with it.

'Seems fair. Tell you what: tell Lars at the livery stable that I said it was OK to give you a horse. Say I'll be by tomorrow to settle up.'

I nodded my thanks. 'I ought to know your name.'

'Forbes. Sheriff Lonnie Forbes. You heard of me?'

I shook my head.

He scowled, disappointed. 'Reckon you can't be from around here.'

Rather than feed his ego, I started for the door.

'Hey, mister — '

I paused and looked at him. 'What?'

'If I need you for anythin', where'll you be?'

'I already told you. Mexico.' I left.

11

Gustafson's Livery Stable was on the other side of the street, facing the railroad. There were no street lights, but the moon was bright enough for me to see that the big double-doors were open. Wanting to get out of town as fast as possible I crossed over and hurried toward the stable.

On the way I passed the Hotel Carlisle, an imposing, two-storey, red-brick edifice financed by railroad money that looked out of place amongst all the adobe and wood-frame buildings surrounding it. Looking at it, I remembered that Sarah was staying there. I knew there was no future for us, but I couldn't stop thinking about her and as an excuse to see her one more time I decided to say goodbye before picking up my horse.

Entering the elegant, gas-lit lobby, I

ignored the disdainful looks that the seated guests gave me and asked the waspish-looking desk clerk for Sarah's room number. He gave me a withering look that said I didn't belong there and said haughtily: 'I'm afraid that's quite impossible, sir. We do not give out the room numbers of the guests. Hotel policy, you know.'

'Sounds reasonable,' I said. 'Reckon I'll just have to kick all the doors in till I find her.'

'Wait,' the clerk exclaimed as I started away. 'Have a seat, please. I'll send someone to tell Miss Eckers that you're here.' He turned to a boy standing nearby who looked like a toy soldier in a fancy red and gold uniform and whispered something to him. The boy hurried off toward the stairs.

I bought a Mexican cheroot and sat in one of the big over-stuffed chairs by the window. The minutes dragged by. I'd smoked half the cigar before Sarah appeared and by then I was restless almost to the point of leaving.

But once I saw her waltzing across the lobby toward me my mood changed. She was all curves in an apple-green dress, and with her dark hair pulled back on one side and hanging loose on the other I had to admit the wait was worthwhile.

I rose to greet her, the envy of every man in the lobby. As she got close I smelled wet violets in her hair and a moment later felt her lips, cool and moist, press against my cheek.

'So ... it *is* you?' she said coyly. 'How flattering to think you remembered where I was staying.'

'I wanted to say so long.'

'You're going away?'

'It's all right. You don't have to pretend to be disappointed.'

'I'm not pretending. When, may I ask?'

'Tonight. Soon as I leave here.'

'Oh dear, and here I got all prettied up thinking we'd dine together.'

'Well ... I reckon I ... if you're hungry, I mean ... I ... could stay long enough to have supper with you.'

'Are you sure? I certainly don't want to hold you up.'

'I'm sure.'

'Wonderful.'

'But I ought to pick up my horse first . . . in case the fella at the livery stable ain't around later.'

'Of course. In fact I'll go with you — that's if you don't mind?'

I shook my head, trying not to sound too eager as I said: 'No, ma'am. I don't mind at all.'

'It's Miss, remember? I'm still not married.'

'I'll try to remember that.'

★   ★   ★

When we entered the livery stable the owner, Lars Gustafson, was pitching hay into one of the rear stalls. The old, gray-bearded Swede was favoring his left leg, which was swollen with gout, and by the stiffness of his movements I guessed he also suffered from arthritis.

He paused and looked our way. 'Sorry, folks,' he said, leaning on the pitchfork. 'I not have room for more horse.'

'That ain't why we're here,' I explained. 'Sheriff told me to see you 'bout buyin' a horse.'

'Sheriff Forbes, he say that?'

I nodded.

Sarah said: 'You *do* sell horses, correct?'

'When I got me horse to sell, sure, missy.'

'Do you have any to sell right now?'

Gustafson scratched his beard with gnarled stubby fingers, as if giving himself time to consider her question. 'Sure t'ing.'

'I'd like to see 'em,' I said, 'so's I can pick out the one I want.'

Gustafson scratched his beard again then leaned the pitchfork against the wall of a stall, turned and painfully limped to the rear door. 'You follow,' he said when we didn't move.

Sarah slipped her hand into mine and

pulled me after the hostler.

Outside in the dark a lighted lantern hung on a hook at the rear of the stables. Gustafson grabbed it and led us toward a small corral containing seven horses.

We moved to the fence from where I studied them. They'd been sleeping and the light from the lantern waked them and made them nervous. They snorted and nickered, nervously pressing against one another. Their restless movements cast weird shadows on the dirt, which seemed to frighten them.

I checked them over carefully. Judging horseflesh is a crapshoot at best and the seller almost always comes out on top. But over the years I've learned enough about horses not to get too badly burned — and anyways, this horse was free, so what did I have to lose?

There were three bays, two sorrels, a buckskin mare and a brownish-gray roan stallion with a black mane and tail and a black-gray face. Leggy and deep-chested, it looked as if it could run to hell and back.

'I'll take the roan,' I pointed.

'Don't you want to ask price first?'

'Nope.'

'He my best horse.'

'That's why I picked him. Bring him out, OK?'

'Sure t'ing.' Grabbing a rope coiled over the fence, Gustafson opened the gate and entered the corral. At once the horses nickered and, as one, ran to the opposite fence. Gustafson turned patiently, twirled the rope overhead and threw the noose at the roan.

It settled neatly over the horse's head and the old hostler pulled it tight.

I expected the roan to buck or maybe even try to get away. Instead, it uttered an angry squeal and charged Gustafson, teeth bared, ears pinned back, eyes red with rage.

Despite his gout and arthritis the old hostler nimbly jumped back out of the corral and slammed the gate shut in time to avoid the roan's teeth.

'Sweet-natured, isn't he?' Sarah said. I chuckled.

She turned to Gustafson. 'Seems to me, that instead of charging my friend for this vicious animal, you should consider paying *him* to take the brute off your hands.'

'You no understand,' Gustafson said. '*Vuelo*, he not try to hurt me. It is his way of playing games.'

'Could've fooled me,' I said. 'He — '

Sarah cut me off. '*Vuelo?*' she repeated. 'What a strange name. Horses can't fly.'

The old Swede smiled. '*Vuelo*, he fly in different way. He run fast as big wind.'

'I'll take him,' I said, adding: 'Oh, and whatever you want for him, tell Sheriff Forbes and he'll give you the money.'

Gustafson eyed me suspiciously. 'He ask you to say this?'

I nodded.

'Said to include a saddle and a bridle too,' Sarah said, slipping me a wink.

Gustafson grumbled under his breath and signaled for us to follow him back into the stables. There, he took a well-used but still serviceable saddle and bridle down from a peg and dropped them at my feet.

'Better throw in a blanket,' I said. 'I don't want to rub his back raw.'

Grudgingly, Gustafson pulled a hand-made white-and brown-patterned Navaho blanket from a shelf, shook the dust from it and tossed it to me. 'Make your mark here,' he said, handing me an old snuff-stained ledger and a chewed pencil stub. 'Otherwise, Sheriff Forbes not pay me.'

I signed my name and returned the ledger. Then I picked up the blanket, saddle and bridle and told Sarah I'd be right back.

She laughed as if I'd said something funny. 'You must be joking, Macahan. I wouldn't miss this for all the peach blossoms in Texas.'

12

Once outside, I draped the blanket and saddle over the gate and, bridle in hand, entered the corral. Gustafson watched me from the fence. I'd expected Sarah to do the same but she followed right behind me, showing no fear of the roan.

I must have looked concerned because she laughed and said: 'Don't worry about me. I could ride before I could walk.'

'You won't have problem with *Vuelo*,' Gustafson assured me. 'Long as you never use spurs, he easy to ride.'

He sounded convincing, but to be honest I still had my doubts. Horse traders like to sell their plug-uglies first and I wasn't sure if Gustafson was trying to steer me away from the roan or telling the truth.

As I crossed the corral toward the

roan, I noticed the old hostler's rope was still looped around its neck, with the loose end trailing in the dirt. Talking softly, I slowly approached the stallion. It had separated itself from the other horses and now turned to face me, its fiery red-rimmed eyes never leaving me. It watched as I picked up the rope, then snorted angrily and pawed at the ground.

'Easy, boy,' I said gently. 'Easy . . . easy . . . '

'The rope's making him nervous,' Sarah said quietly. 'Stand still a moment while I take it off.'

'No,' I said, motioning for her to get back. 'Stay where you are. You go anywhere near that brown devil and he'll bite or kick the daylights out of you.'

Ignoring me, Sarah walked slowly up to *Vuelo*, her voice low and soothing as she tried to calm him.

'For Chris'sake, woman, didn't you hear me?'

'Hush,' she said. 'He's not mean, he's

just scared.' Reaching the roan, she continued to talk softly to it, all the while inching her hand up his arched neck until her fingers touched the noose.

'Shhhh, that's it, that's my handsome boy,' she whispered, gently stroking the horse's lathered neck. 'You don't mind if I take this ugly old rope off you, do you, *Vuelo*? No-o-o, 'course you don't . . . You don't mind at all . . . See, I'll just lift it up over your ears, slowly, like this, and then . . . Easy, boy, easy,' she said as the roan nervously tossed its head, sweat flying everywhere, and bared its big yellow teeth. 'You don't want to bite me. I'm your friend . . . I'm not going to hurt you, *Vuelo* . . . . No . . . I just want to help you. See, like this . . . yes . . . yes-s-s . . . ' Slowly, gently, she eased the noose over the stallion's twitching ears. 'There, that's better, isn't it? Sure . . . Much better . . . ' Rope in hand, she slowly stepped back, still talking soothingly to the wild-eyed, sweating roan.

'He's all yours,' she said, turning to

me. 'Now be gentle with him. Talk nicely to him ... Tell him how handsome he is ... '

I started to say something sarcastic — then I remembered she was a woman and that all women treat animals like they're human and can't understand why men, especially wranglers, don't feel the same way.

But I didn't want to get on her bad side so, keeping calm, I said: 'I don't reckon calling this sonuvagun handsome is goin' to gentle him, Sarah.'

'Sure it will.'

'What makes you so sure?'

'He's a stallion, isn't he?'

For a moment I didn't catch on. Then, as it hit me, I said: 'Hang on. Let me get this straight. You comparin' horses to men?'

'Just male horses.'

'Oh, just 'cause he's a male horse he's vain?'

'You tell me.'

I could have argued with her all day. But time was short, so I let it slide.

Holding the bridle in front of me so *Vuelo* could see it, I slowly approached the irascible roan. Never taking my eyes off him, and ready to jump back if he took a swipe at me, I heard Sarah's voice behind me as she continued to talk softly to the stallion.

When I was close enough to touch him, I paused and held the bridle out to him so he could smell it. Slowly, suspiciously, *Vuelo* touched it with his nose and sniffed.

'That's right,' I said softly, 'get used to its smell . . . See, there's nothin' to worry about. It's just a bridle . . . ' As I talked, I inched the headgear over his ears and with the straps still loose, gently worked the bit between his teeth. He fought me momentarily then let me pry his teeth apart and slide the bit into his mouth.

'Atta boy. Now I'll just tighten these straps . . . ' I buckled the straps into position, lifted the knotted reins over the roan's head and rested them on his back.

I heard Sarah coming up behind me and turned, ready to tell her to go back to the fence. It was then I saw she was carrying the blanket. 'Go bring the saddle,' she said, 'while I get him familiar with this.'

It's strange. I hate being told what to do, especially by women, but for some reason I couldn't figure, I didn't mind as much when Sarah did it.

When I returned with the saddle she had already placed the blanket over *Vuelo*'s back and was talking softly to him in Spanish. The stallion stood there, calm and unafraid, barely flinching when I threw the saddle on it. Without wasting time, I buckled the cinch strap, kneed the roan in the belly to get rid of any excess breath and tightened the strap.

'He likes it when I talk to him in Spanish,' Sarah said. 'Maybe you should try it?'

I had no intention of having a conversation with a horse in any damned language, so I just ignored her and putting my foot in the stirrup swung up into the saddle. I was ready for all kinds of fireworks. But *Vuelo* just twitched his rump and gave a half-hearted, warning buck then settled down.

'Disappointed?' I said, seeing her expression.

'Well,' she admitted, 'I'd be lying if I said I didn't expect a little more fight out of him than that.'

'Expect or hoped?'

She laughed. 'Am I that obvious?'

I let that slide too. I was just grateful that someone else had saddle-broke him. I'd already eaten more than my fair share of dirt. Waiting until Sarah stepped back I started to tap *Vuelo* with my spurs.

'No, no,' Gustafson yelled. 'No spurs, remember?'

I rolled my eyes. 'If I can't kick him up, how the hell am I supposed to get him movin'?'

'With your knees. He obey good that way.'

'Jesus,' I grumbled. 'Just what I need — a pampered horse.'

'Quit complaining,' Sarah chided. 'He's free, remember?'

She had a point. Using my knees, I nudged the roan forward. I half-expected him to buck. Instead, *Vuelo* responded by loping around the corral. He had a long powerful stride and a smooth, rhythmic gait that made me feel like I was sitting in a rocking-chair. I also sensed that the stallion was tireless.

Sarah must have sensed the same thing, because, when I next reined up alongside her, she said: 'I'm no expert when it comes to horseflesh, but I'd be willing to bet that *Vuelo* could outrun most horses.'

I nodded, agreeing with her, then removed my boot from the stirrup closest to her and stretched out my hand. 'Get up behind me. I'll take you back to your hotel.'

'In this dress, that's asking a lot.'

'You can always walk.'

'Don't get lippy,' she warned. Before I could reply, she grasped her dress with both hands, saying: 'Close your eyes.'

I obeyed. I heard her petticoats rustling, felt her grab my hand and put her toe in the stirrup — 'OK, you can look now' — and pulled her up behind me.

'Hang on,' I said. Waiting until she clasped her hands about my waist, I then rode on along the alley beside the stables, out into the street toward the hotel.

13

The dining room in the Carlisle was as fancy as the lobby. Maybe that was the problem. Other than the local Mexicans, the citizens of Santa Rosa were mostly from pioneer stock that by grit, courage and tireless endeavor had become cattlemen, storekeepers or farmers — folks who weren't accustomed to elegant red and gold trappings, white linen tablecloths, ornate silverware and uniformed waiters serving French wine and gourmet cuisine on porcelain dishes.

As a result, Sarah and I had the dining room almost to ourselves. We sat at a table by the window overlooking the street and ate prime rib, roast potatoes and glazed carrots. My meat wasn't burned the way I like it and I couldn't taste the carrots on account of the sugary sauce, but I didn't complain:

sitting across from Sarah, listening to her laugh and watching her eyes sparkle seemed to make eating secondary.

We topped our dinner off with fresh mint ice cream then left the hotel and at Sarah's suggestion, stretched our legs along Main Street. It was dark and there were very few people around. She wore a pale-gray woolen shawl over her bare shoulders but it didn't protect her against the desert chill. Shivering, she insisted I put my arm around her. I didn't put up much of a fight, which seemed to please her, and as we approached the sheriff's office she asked me why I was so intent on going to Mexico. 'Do you have a sweetheart there? Is that why you're deserting me?'

I didn't feel like answering, so shook my head.

'Oh, no,' she said. 'You can't dodge the question by giving me the silent treatment. Tell me the truth: do you have a lady waiting there for you?'

I considered her question for a moment then said truthfully: 'Not waitin' for me, no.'

'Then what makes Chihuahua or anyplace else in Mexico so important that you're willing to ride off and abandon me?'

'I was offered a job,' I said. 'Ramrod for one of the big *hacendados*.'

We'd drawn level with the sheriff's office. Sarah stopped, draped her arms around my neck and stared at me, the moon mirrored in her big green eyes.

'And this important rancher,' she whispered, 'does he happen to have a daughter? I thought so,' she said when I didn't answer. 'And this daughter, who I'm sure is beautiful, is she the real reason you can't wait to ride back across the border?'

'N-No, I — '

'Reason I ask, Macahan, is you don't appear to be the kind of man who'd ride all the way to Mexico just for wages. In fact, I'd say work and you are pretty much strangers.'

I was surprised that she'd pegged me so easily. 'You can tell that by just havin' dinner with me?'

'No. But what I *can* tell — by the lack of calluses on your hands — is you haven't exactly spent your life roping cattle, breaking mustangs or working in the fields like some lowly *campesino*.'

'Maybe I wear gloves,' I said. 'Ever thought of that?'

'Uh-uh. Truthfully, Macahan, I've only had one thought on my mind . . . ' Before I could ask her what it was, she pulled me into the dark alley alongside the sheriff's office and kissed me.

I've been kissed before, but never like Sarah kissed me.

I kissed her back and for a few moments lost track of where I was.

'Still want to go to Mexico?' she asked, finally stepping back.

I had to admit it didn't seem as important as it had a few moments ago.

'Reckon I could wait a few hours,' I began — and stopped as she suddenly grabbed my shooter from its holster and jammed the gun into my belly.

'That's good to hear,' she said,

' 'cause I don't want to have to shoot you.'

Shocked, I gaped at her for a moment before saying: 'W-What the hell are you — ?'

'Shut up!' she snapped. She cocked the hammer back on my Colt, adding: 'If you want to keep breathing, Macahan, listen, don't talk! *Comprende?*'

I nodded numbly.

'Good. Now, keep your hands where I can see them and start walking. No, not that way,' she said as I started for the street, 'we're going in the back way.'

14

The rear entrance of the sheriff's office was locked. With Sarah keeping the Colt pressed against my back, I banged on the door with my fist.

No one responded. I banged again, harder.

Sheriff Forbes's lumbering footsteps approached on the inner side of the door. 'Yeah? Who is it?' he called out sleepily.

'Ezra Macahan. I have to talk to you.'

'Can't it wait till mornin'?'

'Not if you want to get the gold back.'

That got his attention. He slid the bolt back and opened the door.

His towering figure, silhouetted by the lamp light flickering in his office, appeared before us. 'What gold?' he demanded.

Sarah stepped out from behind me,

Colt in hand, saying: 'Keep your hands where I can see them.'

Surprised, the sheriff slowly raised his hands. His hair was uncombed, his shirt rumpled and he'd taken off his boots, making it obvious that he'd been asleep. He'd also removed his gunbelt.

'What the hell do you want?' he asked Sarah.

'Keys to the cells.'

'Not a chance.'

Sarah sighed wearily. 'Sheriff, I've no call to gun you down. But I will if you don't get me those damn keys!'

'Do it,' I told him. 'She means what she says.'

Sheriff Forbes, hands still held high, turned and plodded back to his office.

I followed him, with Sarah right behind me.

Entering his office the sheriff took a ring of keys from his desk drawer and offered them to Sarah.

'Toss 'em to Macahan. Do it!' she barked when he hesitated. 'Or I swear you won't live the night out.'

Reluctantly, he threw me the keys.

'OK,' she told me. 'Open up.'

I obeyed.

When the door to the jail was open, Sarah wagged her gun at us, saying: 'Both of you — inside!'

We entered the jail. Sarah followed, gun trained on us.

The first of the two cells was unlocked. She motioned for us to enter it. When we obeyed, she told me to throw her the keys. I did. She locked our door and then moved to the second cell which contained the Colbert brothers.

Both of them glared through the bars at her.

'Sure took your sweet damn time,' Laird said angrily.

'Yeah,' Sloane added. 'We was startin' to wonder if you hadn't weaseled out on us.'

'Lucky for you, girlie, you didn't,' Laird growled.

Sarah, about to unlock their cell, stopped and stared balefully at him.

'Are you threatening me?'

'No,' Sloane said quickly. ''Course he ain't.'

'I've been threatened before, you know, and it sure sounds like he's threatening me.'

Sloane laughed uneasily. 'You know my brother, Sarah. Always clownin' around. Ain't that right, Laird?'

His brother didn't say anything.

'*Were* you clowning around?' Sarah demanded.

Deep hatred glinted in Laird Colbert's yellow-gray eyes.

'I'm waiting,' she said grimly.

'Will you quit messin' with her an' say yes,' Sloane told Laird.

'Hell yeah,' Laird said through gritted teeth. 'I was just funnin' around, girl.'

'See?' Sloane said to Sarah. 'I told you so. Now, why don't you pay back all the good times I showed you an' unlock that door so we can ride out of here?'

She smiled unpleasantly . . . toying with them for another moment and then unlocked their cell.

It was a mistake.

The Colbert brothers pushed out past her and Sloane started for the door.

Laird didn't. He took a step, wheeled and punched Sarah in the face. She went sprawling, unconscious as she hit the floor.

'What the hell?' Sloane began.

Laird ignored him. Picking up my gun, he went to shoot Sarah. But Sloane grabbed his arm and jerked it upward an instant before Laird pulled the trigger.

'You crazy?' he yelled. 'You kill a woman for no reason an' there won't be a livin' soul from here to hell and back won't shoot us on sight!'

Laird started to argue but Sloane dragged him out of the jail. I heard them grab rifles from the gun-rack and then run out the front door.

'Looks like we're in for a long night,' I said grimly.

The sheriff ignored me. Moving to

the bars, he looked down at Sarah who still lay unconscious on the cement floor.

'Never would've figured she was the kind of gal who'd ride with killers like the Colbert boys.'

I felt the same way. But I was still too mad at Sarah for tricking me to admit it out loud. 'Don't happen to have a spare key in your pocket, do you?'

'Nope. Only extra key's in my desk drawer.' He yawned and sleepily rubbed his eyes. 'Guess we'll have to wait till sunup an' then hope someone happens to stop by.'

'Maybe she'll get it for us,' I said, as Sarah started to come around.

'Would you,' he said, 'after you just helped break out two killers wanted in every state in the southwest?'

He had a point. 'I might,' I said, 'if a certain sheriff offered to put in a good word for her with the circuit judge.'

Sheriff Forbes yawned again as he considered my suggestion.

'I'd be willin' to do that,' he agreed.

'Then now's the time to tell her,' I said as Sarah sat up groggily and gingerly felt her swollen, bloody lip, 'before she remembers that she just broke the law and hightails it out of here.'

15

Once Sarah's head cleared and she was back on her feet Sheriff Forbes quickly explained about the extra key in his desk and how if she'd let us out, he'd ask the judge to be lenient with her.

Instead of being grateful, as I expected, she looked at us defiantly and said: 'But I'd still end up in jail — or maybe even prison, wouldn't I?'

'Possible,' the sheriff admitted.

'So why would I want to do that?'

'It's better than bein' an outlaw,' I said, 'having to spend the rest of your days on the run.'

'Aren't you forgetting something?'

'Like what?'

'If I shoot you both, and say the Colbert brothers did it when they were escaping, who'd know the difference? After all, they're not likely to mention it and as for me, I am a respected schoolteacher, so who'd suspect me of being involved with such ruthless murderers?'

I looked at Sheriff Forbes and realized he was sweating.

'Time to belly up to the bar,' I told him.

He took off his hat and scratched his head. 'Well, I . . . uhm . . . I mean . . . ' He paused and again scratched his head. 'W-What if I — '

'We — '

' — we never said nothing 'bout you bein' here at all?' he asked Sarah. 'That way you couldn't be blamed for the Colbert boys escaping. Would you let us out then?'

Sarah looked at us, long and hard, said: 'Why should I trust you — either of you? Once I let you out, you could change your minds and arrest me for — '

'No, no,' I assured her. 'That'd never happen. Would it, Sheriff?'

'Nope,' he promised. 'Never. I swear.'

'Please, Sarah,' I said. 'Let us out.'

'The longer you keep us locked up,' the sheriff reminded, 'the less chance I have of swearin' in a posse and catchin' up with the Colbert boys.'

Sarah hesitated for another moment before saying: 'All right. I'm probably going to regret this, but . . . ' She unlocked the door to our cell and stepped back so we could get out.

Sheriff Forbes glared at her and momentarily I was worried that he was going to change his mind and arrest her. Then he grabbed the keys from her and hurried out the door to his office.

Sarah studied me briefly and then smiled as if she knew a secret.

'Disappointed?'

'A mite.'

'Never judge a gambler by his smile, Macahan. You'll lose your boots every time.'

'It ain't my boots I'm worried about,' I said, sore that I still cared for her.

'What then?'

I could tell by the look in her eyes that she knew damned well what I was talking about. And that made me even angrier. Deciding that nothing could be gained by discussing my feelings for her, I walked out without another word.

I heard her call my name. But I ignored her and with a quick goodbye nod to Sheriff Forbes, left his office.

Women!

Dammit, did a man ever live long enough to figure them out?

16

Outside, it was dark save for a sickle moon peeking between drifting clouds and the lights glimmering in the windows of the cantinas facing Main Street.

Everyone seemed to have tucked themselves in for the night and as I crossed over to the hotel where I'd tied up the roan, I realized it had gotten bitterly cold. Blaming it on the chilling desert wind blowing northward from the border, I pulled up the collar of my denim jacket and tucked my hands in the pockets.

As I neared the roan I glimpsed movement in the shadowy doorway of Melvin's Haberdashery. I jerked my iron and cautiously approached the store.

'Step out so I can see you,' I said, 'or I'm goin' to start shootin'.'

'You'd be sorry if you did,' replied a voice I recognized.

Holstering my Colt, I waited for Sarah to step into the moonlight.

'What do you want?' I demanded as she approached.

'Still sore at me, huh?'

Even with a swollen lip she looked beautiful in the moonlight. I wanted to grab her and kiss her as hard as I could — which pissed me off even more.

'I asked you a question,' I said.

She stopped in front of me, said only: 'We need to talk.'

' 'Bout what?'

'Not out here.'

'I got nothin' to say to you, Sarah Eckers.'

'But I have something to say to you, Macahan. And you'd be advised to hear me out.' Before I could reply, she turned and hurried into the hotel.

Grudgingly, I trudged after her.

★ ★ ★

116

Upstairs in her hotel room I found her sitting at a table by the window, pouring tequila into two tumblers.

'Close it,' she said as I entered.

I shut the door and took the glass she offered me. She then silently toasted me and gulped down half of her drink. The alcohol stung her split and swollen lips, making her wince.

'I'm going to take a chance on you, Macahan. Maybe I shouldn't, but Marshal Cady trusted you so . . . ' She finished her drink and poured herself another before continuing. 'I've been after the Colbert gang for six months now — '

'After?'

'Yes. A while back I spent some time with them in Puerto Palomas, a little town south of — '

'The border, I know.'

'Before that I'd been tracking them for several months, and finally their trail led me to Mexico. I wouldn't have known they were holed up in Palomas if I hadn't questioned a driver for the Butterfield Stage, whose Mexican wife and family lived in Chihuahua. He told me the gang spent a lot of time drinking and playing poker in a cantina called *El Tecolote*. You know it?'

I nodded.

'Well, I knew I couldn't just walk in there and throw down on them — there were too many other gang members. So I pretended to be a barfly and began cozying up to Sloane — '

' 'Mean you became his woman?'

'Guess you could call it that.'

It was the last thing I wanted to call it. 'So that's what he meant when he told you to pay back all the good times he'd showed you?'

She nodded.

Bristling, I gulped my tequila. I felt it burn my throat as it went down and waited for her to continue.

Instead, she carried her glass to the bed, sat, and stuck her right foot out to me.

'Don't get excited,' she said, reading

my expression. 'The boot's all you get to take off.'

I turned my back to her and gripped the extended boot. She placed her other boot on my backside and pushed as I pulled. After a brief struggle the boot came off and I gave it back to her. She turned it upside down and shook it. Something shiny fell out. She tossed it to me.

I turned it over in my hand. Circular with a star in the middle, the badge had RAILROAD stamped across the top and POLICE on the bottom and in the center the letters: S.P. R.R.

My jaw dropped.

'Obviously, you never suspected,' she said wryly.

'Why would I? You told me you were a teacher.'

'Yes, but I didn't think you believed me. 'Least, your eyes said you didn't.'

Surprised to hear that, I said: 'Why didn't you say somethin' in the jail?'

'I wasn't sure I could trust you.'

'Thanks.'

'Don't get pissy.'

'Hell, if you didn't trust me, you could've at least told Sheriff Forbes.'

'Didn't trust him, either. Still don't.'

'Is there anybody you do trust?'

She said only: 'In my profession, trusting the wrong person can get you killed.'

'You read that somewhere or are you talkin' from personal experience?'

She sighed, the expelled air fluttering her lips, and stared off as if lost in thought. Then in a sad, distant voice, she said: 'There was once this railroad detective — a man called Vincent Flowers. You heard of him?'

'Uh-uh.'

'He's a widower. Has a young son called Violet, of all names. Well, one day he confided in his fiancée . . . told her what he did for a living. A month later he was dead . . . shot to pieces as he boarded a train in San Francisco.' She paused, gulped the last of her tequila and gave another painful sigh. 'Guilt's a funny thing, don't you think?'

I guessed she was referring to herself and had no answer for her.

'You make what at the time sounds like a harmless, innocent remark — my God, I can't even remember what I said or whom I told now — and next thing you know, all your dreams are shattered like broken glass.' She held out her empty tumbler. I picked up the bottle and poured her another drink. She gulped it down like she and tequila were old friends.

'So why're you confiding in me?'

'I told you. Because Marshal Cady trusted you . . . '

'He didn't even know me.'

'Maybe not. But he must've sensed an honesty about you that impressed him.' She gazed into her glass, using her forefinger to stir the tequila around. 'Am I wrong to trust you?'

I shook my head.

'Didn't think so.' She smiled, a sad little smile that echoed with memories, and added: 'Truth is I need your help, Macahan.'

'Ezra.'

'Is that what everybody calls you?'

'Mostly.'

'Then I'll call you Macahan.'

I shot her a look. 'You always this ornery?'

'Mostly,' she said, mimicking my voice.

Normally, I would have laughed. But I had an uncomfortable feeling that I was about to jump into something dangerous; perhaps even fatal.

'This help you need,' I said, 'why do you think I'm your man?'

''Cause I saw the way you handled a gun against the Comancheros.'

That at least made sense. 'What exactly do you want me to do?'

'Help me track down the Colbert gang — specifically the three brothers. They robbed four of our trains and — '

'Sarah, I'm a drifter — a wrangler, at best — not a lawman.'

'If you're willing to raise your right hand, I'll correct that oversight.'

The responsibility of being deputized

chewed through my belly like barbed wire. Fighting down my instinct to say no, I grabbed the bottle, filled my glass and gulped down half the tequila.

'So, what's your answer, Macahan?'

'First, I got to know somethin'.'

'I'm listening.'

'If you're after the Colbert brothers, like you claim, then why'd you let Laird and Sloane go? I mean, if you'd kept them locked up, you'd now only have one brother left to arrest — Judd.'

'I know. But sooner or later he would've found out what I'd done and then he and the rest of the gang would have gone to ground, maybe even holed up in the sierras — which means I'd never catch him.'

'And this way?'

'Odds are he and his brothers will bed down in Palomas. There we've got a chance to round them up ... and bring them back here to stand trial.' She paused and drilled me with a challenging look. 'So ... you in or out?'

'In,' I heard myself say.

She gave a tiny knowing smile that irritated me.

'Dammit, you knew I'd throw in with you, didn't you?'

'Let's say I liked my chances,' she said. 'Now, raise your right hand, Macahan, and repeat after me . . . '

17

The Colbert brothers made it easy for us to follow them.

Wherever they went they left a trail of violent bloodshed. In La Mesilla, a small sun-splashed pueblo known for its cantinas and festivals, Sloane knifed a Mexican bartender for not serving him fast enough; in Blanco Canyon they robbed and killed a prospector for his gold dust; while in the village that would later be called Columbus Laird gunned down the jealous husband of a pretty Flamenco dancer he met in La Cantina de Flores. Then, before the local sheriff and his deputies could arrest them, the brothers kidnapped the dancer and fled to Mexico.

Now, hours later as we approached the border, Sarah reined up her horse and turned to me. 'There's something you ought to know, Macahan.'

'What?'

'Mexico's out of my jurisdiction.'

'Meaning we got no legal authority to arrest anyone, includin' the Colbert gang?'

'Exactly.'

'All the more reason to shoot the bastards.'

'I'm serious.'

'So am I.' I urged the roan forward and he trotted across the border.

* * *

Soon we reached the outskirts of Puerto Palomas, a dangerous, squalid little town that was a haven for outlaws, border trash and the ugliest whores known to man.

With Sarah leading the way, we rode along dusty narrow streets that wound between rundown adobe hovels inhabited by dirt-poor Mexican families. Grubby half-naked children played in the sunbaked dust, while the mothers stood in shady doorways watching us ride past, their dark eyes bright with fear and curiosity.

Finally, we reached the main street that led to the tiny plaza. An eyesore with no boardwalks and littered with trash, the street was full of ruts and flanked on both sides by shabby buildings, many of which were cantinas. Horses were tied up outside them, their sweaty glistening coats indicating they'd been standing in the hot sun for hours. I could hear mariachi music playing inside some of the cantinas, mingled with raucous laughter and singing.

'How do you want to play this?' I asked Sarah as we dismounted outside El Tecolote, an old pink adobe cantina that had an owl painted on the wall above the door.

'The kitchen's in back,' she said, thumbing at an alley that separated the cantina from the next building. 'You come in through that way while I go in the front. If we time it right, hopefully we'll catch them off-guard.'

As we tied up our horses, there was a

sudden roar of laughter inside the cantina. Moments later, the batwing doors burst open and a man was kicked out into the street. He stumbled and collapsed in the dirt, too drunk to get up.

One of the two big bearded men who'd thrown the drunk out tossed his hat after him, while the other man drew his six-gun and shot holes in it.

Sarah and I ducked behind our horses so the men couldn't see us. Almost as drunk as their victim, they kept firing until they had emptied their guns, at the same time yelling obscenities at the drunk. Then punching each other playfully, they staggered back inside.

'Recognize 'em?' I asked Sarah, as she pulled her rifle from its scabbard.

She nodded. 'Mel Casper and Kyle Wolpert — been with the Colbert boys from the outset.'

'Then there's a good chance the rest of the gang are in there with 'em?'

'That'd be my guess.'

Worried about her safety, I said: 'Which means you'll be recognized the minute you walk in.'

'So?'

'So, why don't I go in the front and you take the back? Laird and Sloane might not remember me right away and that'll give us a few seconds' advantage. Might be all we need to get the drop on them.'

Sarah scowled at me. 'Listen, Macahan. I know you mean well, but I give the orders. Not you.'

'Dammit, I wasn't tryin' to give orders. It just makes good sense is all. But, hey, if orders mean more than good sense, go ahead.' Winchester in hand, I started away.

'Macahan.'

Only a few steps into the alley, I paused and looked back at her. 'Yeah?'

'You're right. You go in the front door.'

'Got it.' I watched as she took two pairs of handcuffs from her saddle-bag, hooked them on her belt and walked past me on down the alley.

I knew it had been hard for her to swallow her pride and at that moment I truly respected her.

'Soon as I reach the end of the alley,' she called back to me, 'give me ten seconds before you bust in.'

I nodded.

'You *can* count, right?'

'No, but I can tick off all my fingers.'

Chuckling, she disappeared around the rear of the cantina.

I began counting as I headed for the entrance.

There were two small, hard-looking gunmen, both with low-slung, pegged-down holsters, talking outside the front door. They gave me suspicious stares as I approached, hands drifting down to their guns.

I didn't recognize their faces from any wanted posters I'd seen, and not knowing if they were with the Colbert gang or not I decided not to incite them and put Sarah in even deeper jeopardy. So keeping my eyes lowered, I started to walk around them.

'Hold up, mister,' one gunman said, blocking my path.

'You got business in there?' the other demanded.

I'd already counted to seven, and knew if I didn't get in the cantina within three seconds Sarah might be gunned down. So without bothering to answer, I swung my Winchester at his head, slamming him back against the cantina. Even as he slumped down, unconscious, I kicked the other gunman between the legs. He doubled over, sucking wind, and I whacked him over the head with the rifle. He collapsed in a heap at my feet.

Stepping over him I pushed in through the batwings.

18

My timing was perfect. As I entered the cantina and paused just inside the door, Sarah stepped out of the kitchen, her rifle aimed at the Colbert brothers — Judd, Sloane and Laird — who stood drinking at the bar.

'You three,' she barked at them. 'Don't move!'

The brothers froze for an instant. Then Laird, who'd been pouring himself a drink, slowly set the bottle down and in the same motion, grabbed the six-gun lying on the bar beside him.

Sarah fired, twice. The first bullet splintered the bar inches from his hand, the second knocked his Colt to the floor.

'Move again,' she warned him, 'and you're dead.'

Laird glared at her. Then, sensing that he'd better not press his luck, stood very still. Beside him, his two brothers did the same.

Meanwhile, I'd covered the four gunmen who were playing poker at a corner table. They were large, cruel-eyed men, made all the meaner-looking by soiled clothing and a week's stubble. I recognized their faces from wanted posters and knew they were part of the Colbert gang.

'Keep your hands where I can see 'em,' I snapped, ''cause unlike the lady here, I won't give you a second chance.'

The gunmen stared hatefully at me and kept their hands on the table.

But their hatred was nothing compared to the hatred in Judd's narrowed gray eyes as he glared at Sarah. 'You're goin' to be sorry for this,' he growled. 'Sorrier than you ever figured possible.'

'Could be,' she admitted. 'But at least I won't be rotting in prison or hanging from a rope while I'm feeling sorry.'

'You can't arrest us,' Sloane said angrily. 'Down here Mexican law's the only law that counts.'

'I'll remember that,' Sarah said, 'when I'm taking you back across the border. Meanwhile, all three of you unbuckle your gunbelts and put your hands on the bar. Now!' she snapped when they didn't move. She fired another shot, the bullet splintering the bar between Sloane and Judd, causing both men to flinch and quickly obey her.

When the brothers had dropped their gunbelts, Sarah took a pair of handcuffs from her belt and snapped one cuff on Sloane's left wrist, the other on Laird's right. She then cuffed Judd's hands behind his back with the second pair.

'What about these four?' I asked, indicating the poker players.

'Shoot them,' she said coldly.

'Just like that?'

'You questioning my orders?'

'Uh-uh.'

'Then pull the damn trigger!'

I sensed she was bluffing but couldn't be sure. I faced the gunmen, who now looked panicky, and aimed at the nearest man.

'Wait,' Sarah said, 'I have a better idea.' She turned to the gunmen. 'Here are your choices: he shoots you. I take you back to the States, along with your cohorts, where you'll hang. Or you can stay here and finish your game. Your call.'

'One last thing,' I added before they could reply, 'we can't stop you from following us, but I'm warnin' you: the first time I see any of you — or even *think* I see any of you behind us, no matter how far away, I'll kill one of the Colbert brothers. We clear on that?'

None of the gunmen responded.

'I *said* — are we clear on that?'

As one, the four men nodded.

'Good.' I grinned, dimples and all. 'Now, what's your poison?'

The gunmen swapped uneasy looks, nodded in silent agreement and then the man nearest me said: 'We'll stay in here.'

'Good call,' I said. 'Now, drop your guns.'

Grudgingly, they obeyed.

I kicked each gun across the room. Then keeping the gunmen covered with my rifle, I joined Sarah.

'Whenever you're ready.'

She prodded the brothers with her Winchester, saying: 'Move.'

Reluctantly, the three of them walked ahead of her to the door. I backed up behind her, never taking my eyes off the four gunmen.

At the door I paused and told them: 'Remember what I said, gents. One of you so much as shows his face outside this cantina, better bring a shovel, 'cause you'll have to bury a Colbert.'

Their eyes glittered with fury, but none of them moved.

I backed out of the batwings after Sarah.

19

The shots she'd fired inside the cantina had been ignored by the men and women on the dark, unlighted street — proving just how immune the townspeople had become to the law-lessness that was rampant in the unruly border town.

I joined Sarah in the street outside the cantina, and while she kept her rifle trained on the doors, ready to shoot any of the gunmen who came after us, I helped the Colbert brothers get mounted.

Judd posed no problem. All he needed was a boost from me. But his brothers were a different story. Because they were cuffed together, every time Laird or Sloane tried to put a foot into the stirrup they pulled each other off-balance, causing them to stumble and fall to the ground.

Their angry cussing and failed attempts to get mounted unnerved their already jittery horses. The animals kept snorting and rearing up, jerking their heads in an effort to break the reins loose from the tie-rail.

Not wanting to attract any additional attention from the passersby, I grabbed both saddle horns and pulled the horses close together, making it possible for Laird and Sloane to finally get mounted. I then swung up onto *Vuelo* and signaled to Sarah that we were ready to leave.

Giving the cantina doors a final look, she tucked her rifle into its scabbard, stepped into the saddle and rode over to me. Once she was alongside I grabbed the reins of the outlaws' horses, wheeled *Vuelo* around and forgetting Lars Gustafson's advice, dug my spurs into the roan.

Instead of moving forward, as I'd expected, the irascible stallion reared up in a fury, unseating me.

An instant later gunfire came from

the alley beside the cantina.

There's no doubt I would have been shot, possibly even killed if the roan hadn't reacted to my spurring. But, as the ground slammed the breath out of me, I wasn't thinking of thanking him — just shooting whoever was in the alley.

Rolling over, I grabbed my dropped rifle and fired several times in the direction of the shots. The alley was too dark to see anyone, but a sharp yelp told me I'd hit at least one of my attackers.

Sarah, meanwhile, had reined up and was also firing into the alley. I heard another cry and a man stumbled forward and collapsed on his face. It was one of the two gunmen who'd braced me earlier outside the cantina.

Jumping up, I charged into the alley — firing as I ran.

The flashes from my Winchester showed the body of the other gunman slumped down against one wall. There was blood on his shirt over his heart and foam dribbled from his mouth. I bent over him and looked into his bloodshot eyes, just as he took his last breath.

Before I could relax, though, I heard gunshots behind me followed by a cry of pain from Sarah. I ran back into the street and saw her slumped over the neck of her horse — and, behind her, the shadowy outlines of the Colbert brothers galloping off.

I quickly fired after them, but hit nothing but darkness.

20

I desperately wanted to pursue them, but I knew helping Sarah was more urgent. Running to her horse, I gently lifted her from the saddle and set her on the ground. She'd been shot in the left shoulder, just below the collar bone, and was bleeding through her shirt. Her eyelids fluttered and she looked questioningly at me.

'It's OK,' I assured her. 'I'll take care of you.'

I don't know if she understood, or even heard me, but she seemed to smile; then her eyes closed and she went limp.

I heard voices and looked up. A crowd of onlookers had gathered around us. Most of them were *campesinos* clad in white cotton, the men clasping big straw sombreros, the women clad in bright clothing. All of them looked frightened and from what I'd heard, they lived in fear of the bullying gunmen and outlaws who ruled their town.

'Doctor? Doctor?' I yelled at them. '*Donde esta el medico?*'

A small, dark-skinned young man timidly replied that the doctor lived at the end of the street. As if to make sure I understood him, he pointed at a modest whitewashed adobe house that faced the livery stable and blacksmith shop. By squinting I could vaguely make the house out in the darkness.

'*Alli! Alli!*' the young man said. '*En la casa blanca!*'

Thanking him, I picked Sarah up and carried her toward the white house. Behind me the young man took it upon himself to bring our horses.

Sarah was bleeding badly. I walked as fast as I could and was panting by the time we reached the house. The young man, who'd said his name was Eduardo Sanchez, tied up the horses and pounded on the door. It was opened by a tall, thin, dignified-looking man with thick white hair and drooping white mustaches. He peered inquiringly at us, holding up a hurricane lamp in order to see our faces.

Eduardo spoke rapidly to him. I don't speak Spanish fluently but I know enough to know he'd described what had happened. The doctor, whose name was Jore Herrera, didn't hesitate. Grasping my arm, he motioned for me to enter.

I carried Sarah into the house. The sparsely furnished living area was lit by fluttering candles. As I gently put Sarah on the table I noticed an elegant, sad-eyed woman dressed in mourning black watching us from a doorway leading to the bedrooms.

The doctor spoke to her. I didn't catch what he said, but the woman took a kettle from the stove, filled a basin with hot water and brought it to the table.

Meanwhile the doctor handed me the lamp and bent over Sarah. I held the lamp close so he could see what he was doing. Gently unbuttoning Sarah's bloodstained shirt, he peeled back the side covering her wound. She winced and moaned softly . . . briefly opened her eyes . . . then fainted.

Dr Herrera moved quickly. Washing his hands, he dried them on the towel held by the woman. She hadn't spoken yet but by the respectful, loving way she looked at the doctor and obeyed his commands, I guessed she was his wife.

The doctor leaned over Sarah and examined the wound. With each beat of her heart blood welled from the bullet hole. Dr Herrera said something to the woman, who quickly fetched a black leather bag from a cupboard and brought it to him.

'Is she goin' to be OK?' I asked as he took out a pair of forceps.

Ignoring my question, he told me to remove the glass chimney. When I did, he held the forceps briefly in the flame and then bent over Sarah again. Next he told me to hold her firmly, adding that it could go badly for her if she moved. I set the lamp down, put my hands on Sarah's shoulders and pressed down on her.

Satisfied, Dr Herrera went to work. It took some probing around to find the bullet. But he worked quickly so that Sarah wouldn't lose much more blood, and finally pulled the slug out then dropped it in a small metal tray.

'Tequila,' he told the woman.

She'd already anticipated his need, and handed him a half-full bottle.

He poured it liberally over the wound before taking a swig himself.

Meanwhile, the woman took a small hunting knife from the bag and held the blade over the flame. When the steel glowed bright orange she handed the knife to the doctor, who used it to cauterize Sarah's wound. Her flesh sizzled, a wisp of smoke curled up and the bleeding stopped. Though unconscious, Sarah grunted, shuddered, and then went limp.

'What are her chances now?' I asked the doctor.

'Better than before I remove the bullet,' he said. He took another swig of tequila then offered me the bottle.

I drank, felt the tequila burn down my throat and returned the bottle.

Dr Herrera took another swallow before saying: 'It is best if the señora — '

' — señorita — '

' — rest for a few days.'

'And then?'

'She should not ride too far. This is possible?' he asked, seeing my frown.

'If you know somewhere we can stay, sure,' I said.

He thought a moment then motioned for me to follow him. I did. He led me into a small bedroom at the rear of the house. It contained a single bed that hadn't recently been slept in, a chest-of-drawers on which sat a sepia-colored photograph of a handsome young boy and a closet full of neatly arranged boy's clothes.

'The *señorita*, she may stay here,' Dr Herrera said.

'Thanks, that's real generous of you, Doc. But what about the boy, there?' I pointed at the photo. 'How's he goin' to feel about giving up his room?'

Dr Herrera's face clouded sadly. 'My son, he does not need it anymore.'

'Oh, is he away at school or somethin'?'

'No, *señor*. Carlos . . . he is now in God's arms.'

'He's dead?'

'*Sí*. Killed by a stray *gringo* bullet meant for someone else.'

I felt like a cold fist had punched me in the gut. 'I'm real sorry,' I said, looking at the boy's photo. 'I can only imagine how painful that must be.'

'It's left a hole in my heart that refuses to heal,' Dr Herrera said. Eyes welling with tears, he nodded politely to me and left.

21

For the next three days Sarah was too weak to get out of bed. She slept most of the time, only waking when Dr Herrera changed her dressing or to eat a little of the hot broth I brought her.

On the fourth morning, she felt strong enough to get up for a few hours. She was restless and on edge, and though Dr Herrera kept saying how pleased he was by how fast her wound was healing, it wasn't healing fast enough for Sarah. She desperately wanted to go after the Colbert brothers and became frustrated when she found that she barely had the strength to walk without my help, let alone ride.

I tried to calm her, assuring her that she'd be much stronger in a few days, but it didn't help. Her nerves were strung out and she snapped at everything I said. I didn't call her on it, figuring that she'd get over it once she felt better. But the next day she was even more irritable, and the following evening all hell broke loose when Eduardo showed up and said that he'd heard the Colbert gang was leaving town in the morning.

'Dammit to hell,' she exclaimed. 'I've finally got them in my sights and now they're taking off and I'll have to track them down all over again.'

'Maybe not,' I said. Then to Eduardo: 'Do you know where they're headed, *amigo*?'

'No, señor. But I have heard — how you say it — *susurros en el viento* — '

'Whoa,' I said, thinking I'd misunderstood him. 'Whispers on the wind?'

'*Sí, señor.*'

Sarah and I swapped puzzled looks. About to question him further, it suddenly hit me what he meant.

'Rumors — is that what you're tryin' to say?'

'*Sí, sí,* rumors . . . '

'And these rumors,' Sarah put in,

'what do they speak of?'

'Santa Rosa.'

'Santa Rosa?' She looked at me. 'The whole gang's wanted in New Mexico. Why would they risk going there?'

'I don't know.' I turned to Eduardo. 'Why do you think folks are talking about Santa Rosa?'

'It is to here that I believe the gang rides, *señor*.'

'Why there?' Sarah asked.

'Forgive me, *señorita*. This, the whispers did not tell me.'

'It's OK,' I said. 'You did fine, *amigo*. Now you better go. And be sure to leave by the back door. We don't want anyone gettin' suspicious 'bout why you keep coming here, or else word could leak back to the Colbert brothers and they might decide to swap lead with us.'

'Let 'em come,' Sarah said grimly. 'It'll save us the trouble of going after them later.'

'True,' I said. 'But 'later' you won't have a gimpy wing and more importantly, we won't run the risk of gettin'

Dr Herrera or his wife gunned down.'

That stung. 'My God,' she said, ashamed. 'How could I be so selfish to forget about them?'

'Stop beating on yourself,' I said. 'It ain't a matter of bein' selfish, it's a matter of widening your vision. Hell, you been focused on the Colbert brothers' trail so long, you lost sight of the horizon.'

She smiled wryly. 'Thanks for letting me off the hook, as my dad used to say. But I'm a big girl now and big girls have to bite the bullet. But I promise you, Macahan, I won't lose sight of the horizon again.' Turning to Eduardo, she added: 'If you hear any more 'whispers' about Santa Rosa . . . or why the Colbert gang's headed there, let me know right away. *Comprende?*'

'*Sí, señorita.*' He turned to me. 'I go now, Señor Macahan.'

'*Vaya con Dios, amigo.*' We shook hands. I waited for him to duck out the back door before saying to Sarah: 'Got any ideas?'

She wearily shook her head, fatigued by all the excitement. 'Nada. You?'

'Uh-uh.'

'Well, one thing's for sure: the Colberts definitely aren't going to Santa Rosa for the waters.'

'A hold up, maybe?'

'Bank, you mean?'

'Bank — Express Office — maybe even a train if it's carrying gold.'

'How would they know that? Gold shipments are kept secret. The railroad doesn't even tell the engineer until the last minute. I know: I've ridden shotgun on those trains.'

I thought a moment. 'What about kinfolks?'

'Elaborate, please.'

'What if the engineer was a relative or a friend of someone in the gang? Even if he was told about the gold just before the train took off, he'd still have time to use the telegraph.'

'Possibly,' she admitted. 'But the trouble with that theory is Palomas doesn't have a telegraph office. And neither do any of the other villages this side of the border. So the gang couldn't get the message, no matter who sent it. As for the bank in Santa Rosa, from what I've heard, unless there are cattle buyers in town they don't keep enough money in the vault to make it worthwhile robbing.'

'Then it's got to be the train,' I said. 'Either that or somethin' we ain't even figured on.'

Sarah had stopped listening. 'I must get there before them.'

'Where — Santa Rosa?'

'No. The village just across the border. There's a telegraph at the station.'

'Are you *loco*? You can barely walk, remember?'

'But I can sit in a wagon.'

'A wagon? Where the hell we goin' to find a wagon at this hour? An' even if we knew where one was, how would we get it? If I show myself on the street and one of the Colberts recognizes me, it's not only the end of the trail for us but maybe the doc and his wife, too.'

Sarah smiled, like a gambler with a royal flush. 'No act is random.'

'What?'

'Life. Everything happens for a purpose.'

'What's that, another of your old man's pearls of wisdom?'

'No.'

'Then get to the meat, dammit.'

'The 'meat',' she said, 'is that I've been lying in bed for days like a caged tiger, looking out the window and feeling sorry for myself, and all the time it's been sitting there, staring me in the face.'

'What has?'

'A wagon. There's one for sale across the street. Outside the blacksmith's. He must be really anxious to sell it, too, 'cause every day he keeps lowering the price. If I give Dr Herrera the money, he can go buy it. Then we can hitch our horses to it and leave tonight. We'll keep to the outskirts and dress like *campesinos* and chances are, no one will even notice us.'

Before I could admit it wasn't a bad idea, Dr Herrera knocked and entered.

'*Que pasa?*' he asked, seeing our expressions.

Sarah and I quickly explained what was wrong and asked him if he would buy the wagon for us.

'Of course,' he replied. 'It would be my honor to help you. But I must warn you, *señorita*, if you leave tonight, even by wagon, you face the risk of tearing your stitches. And if that happens, your wound will reopen and you'll start bleeding again . . . I know this is not what you want to hear,' he said, seeing her tight-lipped expression, 'but as a doctor it is my obligation to tell you the truth. And the truth is, *señorita*, you have already lost a lot of blood and this time, you will very likely bleed to death.'

'What if we waited another day or two?' I asked.

'Every day of rest will help,' Dr Herrera said. 'But it is my advice that you rest here for three . . . maybe four more days.'

'Impossible,' Sarah said.

'Are you in such a hurry to die, *señorita*?'

'He *is* the doctor,' I reminded her. 'Might be wise to listen to him.'

'I *have* been listening,' she snapped. 'But all gifts don't come wrapped in pink ribbons. Sometimes reality arrives in a plain old box. And the reality here is, if I don't warn Sheriff Forbes in Santa Rosa that there may be some kind of holdup or robbery in the next day or two, and a bunch of people are killed in the shootout, I could never live with myself. Surely you can understand that, Doctor?'

'Of course,' he said.

'So you'll buy the wagon for us?'

He nodded, a kind, gentle, distinguished-looking gent whose feet were about to take him where his heart didn't want to go.

'One last thing,' I said. 'I hate to ask you to lie for us, Doc, but if it wouldn't trouble your conscience too much it'd be real helpful if the blacksmith thought you were buying it for yourself.'

'That way,' Sarah added, 'it's less likely that the Colberts will get wind of what we're doing.'

'It shall be as you ask,' Dr Herrera said. 'As for my conscience,' he added with a wry smile, 'do not fret over it. Though I manage to present a pure and dignified image to my patients, this would not be the first lie I have ever told. Nor will it be the last.' With a polite bow, he turned and left the room.

'I don't know about you,' I said to Sarah, 'but bein' around that man makes me feel kind of humble.'

'I was thinking the exact same thing,' she said. 'Like you're in the presence of someone noble.'

22

That night, with a wafer-like moon peering between drifting clouds to guide us, Sarah and I set out in the old freight wagon that earlier Dr Herrera had parked behind his house. We did our best to thank him for all he and his wife had done for us, but I knew it wasn't nearly enough; and as we drove away, along a narrow dirt street that wound through the outskirts, we both agreed that one day we'd find a better way to truly repay their kindness.

Everything went smoothly. Wearing borrowed serapes and sombreros, we aroused little attention from the locals we passed. They had their own troubles to contend with and weren't interested in ours. Soon, Palomas disappeared into the darkness behind us and we approached the border. All was quiet. There were no fences or border guards, merely a sign stating we were now entering the USA, and we crossed without mishap. But as we rode on, we heard gunshots behind us.

Reining up, we looked back and saw Eduardo galloping toward us, firing into the air.

Wondering what was wrong, we waited for him to catch up. As he got close I could see he was upset and before we could question him, he blurted out that Dr Herrera had been killed.

'That's impossible,' I said. 'We just left him.'

'*Sí* . . . *sí* . . . . This I know, *señor*. But they hide and watch you. And after you leave, they break into house and — and drag doctor outside — '

'They — who's they?' demanded Sarah.

'*Los forajidos, señorita!*'

'Outlaws?' I said. 'What outlaws? The Colbert brothers, you mean?'

'*Sí, sí, los hermanos de Colbert* — they take them both, El Dr Herrera

and Señora Herrera, and . . . and . . . '
He was too distraught to find the right
words.

'*En Español*,' I told him. '*Hablar en
Español.*'

'*Los castigan y disparar contra ellos
para cobjiar*,' he blurted.

'Those gutless bastards!' I said to
Sarah. 'As payback for sheltering us, the
Colberts shot Dr Herrera and his wife.'

'N-No, that can't be!' Horrified, she
turned to Eduardo. 'Are you sure about
this?'

'*Sí, señorita*. Most sure I am.'

'Where are they now?' I asked. 'Do
you know?'

'*Sí* . . . *sí* . . . hanging outside El
Tecolote so all may spit on them.'

Confused, I said: 'Why are the
Colbert brothers hanging — ?'

'No, no, *señor*. Not *los hermanos*. *El
Dr Herrera y su esposa.*'

His words raged through my mind.
God knows I'm not a bloodthirsty man.
But just then I knew the only thing that
would ever satisfy me or erase that

godawful image was gut-shooting the Colbert brothers ... and watching them slowly die.

I looked at Sarah. I'd seen her angry before, but never like this. Her eyes were two dark-green slits that seethed with rage.

'Turn the wagon around,' she said grimly.

'Jesus, Sarah, you're in no condition to — '

'Either turn this damned wagon around, Macahan, or get the hell off it and I'll drive myself.'

The muzzle of her Colt poked out from under her serape.

I didn't know if she was bluffing, but the look on her face told me not to test her. Shrugging, I turned the wagon around and headed for the border.

Neither of us spoke again. There was no need to. We both knew what the other was thinking. And we both knew what we had to do next.

23

Once we'd crossed the border Sarah told Eduardo to ride ahead of us and warn everyone he trusted to stay in their houses.

'But, señorita — '

'Don't argue with her, *amigo*,' I said. 'Just do as she says. *Comprende?*'

He nodded glumly. 'This I will do,' he promised. 'But after that, I help you kill these *cabrons*.'

'No,' said Sarah. 'Killing's our job. Yours is to make sure there are no innocent people on the street when the shooting starts.'

'We'll give you a few minutes' head start,' I added, 'then we'll be comin' in.'

Eduardo nodded. '*Que Dios este con vosotros, mis amigos.*'

'May God be with *all* of us,' I said.

'Amen,' Sarah breathed.

We watched as Eduardo spurred his

horse ahead, soon swallowed up by the darkness shrouding the town. Then we tossed the sombreros and serapes into the back of the wagon and made sure our guns were fully loaded.

'How do you want to play this?' I asked. 'Same as we did in El Tecolote?'

'No,' Sarah said bitterly. 'No back-door-front-door trickery this time. We meet these bastards head-on.'

'Last man standing?'

'Exactly.'

'What about prisoners?'

'*No tomar prisioneros!*'

'That suits me. But how's killing everyone goin' to sit with your bosses at the railroad?'

Her answer was to take something small and shiny from her pocket and toss it away.

'Any more questions, Macahan?'

'Just one: does this mean I'm no longer employed?'

'Dammit, quit clowning around!'

'Just tryin' to keep you loose.'

'Don't worry about me,' she said

grimly. 'You just get us to El Tecolote; I'll handle the rest.'

'Would that be before or after you maybe bleed to death?'

'Either way,' she said coldly, 'it's no longer your business.'

That cut deep. Reining up, I threw the lines in her lap and jumped down from the wagon.

'Where you going?' she demanded.

'Like you just told me: it's no longer your business.' Cradling my rifle, I began walking toward the center of town.

'Macahan!'

I kept walking.

'Macahan, wait! Please!'

I looked back at her. 'For what — more insults?'

She took a deep breath. 'I'm sorry. I was out of line talking to you like that.'

That helped, but I was still pissed. I kept walking.

'I need you, Macahan,' she said. 'I can't do this on my own.'

Most of my anger melted away. I

stopped and looked back at her. In the pale silvery darkness I could see she was hurting.

'If you don't take it easy,' I said, 'you won't be around long enough to do anythin'.'

'That's why I need you,' she said, 'to make sure this ends tonight.'

'What if I gave you my word to stick around no matter how long it takes — would you wait until we at least stop and rest up for a spell?'

She gave a long, frustrated sigh. 'Macahan, listen to me. I know you mean well. But I can't stop now. We're too close. We've got to take care of the Colberts tonight or tomorrow latest. It might be our last chance before they cross the border and get lost in the *sierras*.'

I knew it was no use arguing with her so I returned to the wagon and climbed up on the box beside her. Grabbing the lines I snapped them over the backs of the horses and they surged forward. That's when I saw her badge glinting on the ground.

'Leave it there,' she said as I started to rein up. 'This isn't railroad business, it's strictly personal.'

I felt the same way. Resting my rifle across my knees, I drove on.

24

Eduardo had done his job well. When Sarah and I entered the outskirts of Palomas the narrow winding streets were deserted.

There wasn't much happening anywhere else either. As we neared the center of town I glimpsed a few dark-eyed faces peering curiously out of windows and darkened doorways. But none of them posed any threat, so I ignored them and kept my eyes trained on the buildings on both sides of the street. It wasn't necessary. No one suspicious was lurking there either.

Now and then I glanced at Sarah, wondering how she was feeling. It was impossible to tell. Her grim jut-jawed expression never changed, not even when we rode over ruts and bumps, the old wagon creaking and rattling in protest.

When we reached the main street it too was empty save for an old drunk staggering past a corral, several horses tied up outside the cantinas and a gaunt yellow mutt digging for scraps among a pile of garbage.

Ahead, on our left, El Tecolote occupied the next corner. I expected to see the bodies of Dr Herrera and his wife hanging outside the cantina, but there was no sign of them and I figured that the locals must have taken them down. In their place stood two horses and a burro tied up outside the entrance.

'Looks like the Colberts already flew the coop,' I said.

'I'll only believe that after we've looked inside,' Sarah said.

I reined up outside the grain and feed store opposite the cantina and tied the lines around the brake. Then, jumping down, I walked around the wagon and helped Sarah down.

She grimaced with pain and I could feel the wetness that had soaked through her shirt. I looked at my right hand and saw it was red with blood.

'You're bleedin' again.'

'That's from earlier — before the doctor looked at me.'

I knew she was lying but didn't press her.

'Why don't I go in first and take a looksee?' I offered.

She didn't bother to answer. Levering a round into her Winchester, she crossed over and walked painfully to the cantina. Silently cursing her stubbornness, I hurried ahead of her and poked open the batwing doors with the butt of my rifle.

The cantina was almost empty. Three misfits drinking at the bar turned toward us, curious to see who was entering. Behind the bar the barkeep, a half-breed big enough to block out the sun, stopped drying a shot glass and also looked our way.

'*Que pasa?*' he said as he saw our rifles.

'The Colbert brothers?' Sarah demanded.

'Where are they?'

He shrugged his massive shoulders. '*No hablar Ingles.*'

Sarah fired. Her bullet barely missed his shoulder and shattered the large, ornate wall-mirror behind him. He stumbled aside, cursing as broken glass showered over his huge lumpy body.

Simultaneously, the three men at the bar ducked and scattered in different directions, all reaching for their six-shooters.

I fired a shot into the ceiling that froze them. 'Keep out of this,' I warned.

They glared at me but left their irons holstered.

Sarah moved to the bar, steadied herself with one arm and aimed her Winchester at the mountain-sized bartender.

'I'm only going to ask you once more, *Gordo*. Where are the Colberts?'

'They leave town,' he replied sullenly.

'When?'

'One, two hour ago maybe.'

'Where're they headed — Santa Rosa?'

'This they not tell me. I swear,' he added fearfully as she started to squeeze the trigger. 'But maybe he know,' he pointed.

Sarah and I turned toward a stubbly-faced man playing solitaire at a table in the corner. He didn't look up but I recognized him instantly: it was Luke Cassidy, the gunman I'd met at the stagecoach way station, Cactus Wells.

25

I gave Sarah my rifle, told her to stay where she was and approached the table. I moved slowly, making sure my hand wasn't near my gun and, when I was within a few steps, Cassidy looked up and studied me with curious, gray-green eyes.

'Thought that might be you,' he said quietly. 'Macahan, isn't it?'

I nodded, glad that he remembered me. 'If you got a moment, Mr Cassidy — '

'Luke — '

'Luke, I'd like to ask you a question.'

'Shoot.'

'Barkeep seems to think you might know where the Colbert brothers are?'

'If I did, *amigo*, I wouldn't be sittin' here. What's your interest in them?' he added before I could say anything.

'We aim to take them back across the

border and watch 'em dangle from a rope.'

'Thought you told me you weren't a lawman?'

'I'm not. But the woman is,' I said, thumbing at Sarah. 'I'm just helpin' her, temporary-like.'

Cassidy frowned at Sarah as if surprised. 'Said she was a school teacher.'

'I know. Told me the same thing. Truth is she's a railroad dick.'

'Be damned.'

'My thought exactly.' I chuckled mirthlessly. 'She's a pistol, all right.'

'I'll bet.' Cassidy went on playing, putting a queen of hearts on a king of spades. 'Wish I could help you, Macahan. I'm lookin' for the Colberts myself, but for a more personal reason.'

'Mind if I ask what it is?'

'They cut up my kid brother in Amarillo and fed his liver to their dogs.'

'Any reason in particular?'

''Cause they could. When you're pure mean that's reason enough.'

Remembering what had happened to Dr Herrera and his wife, I knew he was right. I started to make a suggestion then changed my mind.

'Somethin' else you want to ask me?'

I shrugged. 'I was thinkin' . . . wondering if we might help each other.'

Cassidy made no attempt to answer me. He put a six of clubs atop a seven of diamonds, transferred a red five from another column and then turned up a deuce of hearts. He placed it atop a three of spades and continued going through the deck without finding another card that fitted anywhere. He sighed and shook his head.

'I hate cheatin' at cards.'

'Then don't.'

'I hate losin' worse.'

'I won't tell.'

He grinned and with startling suddenness threw the deck in the air, jerked his Schofield and fired at the falling cards.

One card was punched away from the others. I bent and picked it up. A bullet hole pierced the center of the ace of spades. Impressed, I gave a low whistle.

'Lucky shot,' Cassidy said, putting the ace on the deuce of hearts.

I knew better.

'Sarah an' me,' I said, 'we could use that kind of luck.'

'You asking for my help?'

'I'm sayin' we wouldn't turn you down if you were to offer.'

'Better get her say-so first,' he said, holstering his gun. 'Having someone like me along might offend her principles.'

'I doubt it.' I waved Sarah over. 'She'd ride with the devil himself if it meant throwin' a rope over the Colberts. But just to set you at ease, let's ask her.'

26

I was right. Sarah was glad to have Cassidy ride with us — so long as he let her call the shots. He agreed without argument, which surprised me, and after we'd washed the dust from our throats with a beer, we left the cantina and headed for the border.

A wind had chased the clouds away and the wafer-like moon turned the night bright as day. None of us was in the mood to talk, and save for the yowling of distant coyotes the only sound was the rhythmic plodding of Cassidy's horse and the brittle creaking and jingling of the old freight wagon. Now and then I glanced at Sarah to see if she was in pain. I couldn't tell. She seemed to have stopped bleeding and sat there staring straight ahead, her grim, tight-lipped expression never changing, making it impossible for me to know if she was hurting or feeling faint.

Shortly we crossed the border. Entering the windy, dust-caked pueblo that years later would be called Columbus, we followed the railroad tracks to the little yellow-and-brown station-house. It was closed. A train schedule pinned to the door said the first train was due to arrive at 8:35 from El Paso.

Sarah didn't say anything but for the first time she showed emotion — as disappointment creased her face.

'Unhitch the horses,' she told me.

'Dammit, Sarah, you heard what Dr Herrera said — if that wound of yours reopens, you could bleed to death.'

She didn't argue. She didn't even look at me. Her answer was to slowly, painfully, climb down from the wagon. Cassidy, who was closest, dismounted and went to help her. She ignored his hand and once on the ground, started to unhitch her horse.

Her stubbornness infuriated me. I wanted to grab her and shake some sense into her. Instead, I gently but firmly shouldered her aside, unhitched her horse and led it to the rear of the wagon. Her saddle and blanket lay in back. Grabbing them, I saddled her horse and then helped her mount.

'Thank you,' she said, still not looking at me.

I was too angry to respond. Meanwhile, Cassidy had unhitched my horse and I quickly saddled *Vuelo*. As if annoyed because I made him pull the wagon, the roan stallion tried to bite me. I jumped back, cursing him, and grabbed my Winchester from the wagon box. I then stepped up into the saddle, swung the roan around and rode in the direction of Santa Rosa.

Within moments, Cassidy caught up to me with Sarah not far behind.

'You're right,' he said softly. 'She surely is a pistol.'

★ ★ ★

Dawn was still two hours away when we reached Santa Rosa. None of the stores or cantinas was open and Main Street and Lower Front Street were empty, giving the impression that the town was sleeping peacefully.

Sarah reined up at the first corner, across from Melvin's Haberdashery and said that she'd meet us shortly at the sheriff's office.

'Where you goin'?' I asked.

'Sheriff's house.'

'Alone?'

'After what happened in the jail, I thought maybe the three of us together might spook him — especially when I tell him the bank or the train may be robbed.'

'Remember, you don't have your police badge anymore,' I reminded.

'No, but I still got my ID. That's more than enough identification to satisfy the sheriff.'

'Unless he's in on it,' Cassidy said.

Sarah shot him a look. 'You got a reason to believe he might be?'

'I heard tell he was retiring soon.'

'You'll have to speak plainer than that.'

'Forty a month an' found don't add up to much of a nest egg.'

'But a share of a hold-up would, that it?' I said.

Cassidy shrugged. 'Just a thought.'

'I've heard a lot of things about Sheriff Forbes, some good, some not so good,' Sarah said. 'But never that he was a thief.'

'Ain't sayin' he is,' Cassidy said.

'Then what are you sayin'?' I demanded.

'Just . . . why play your trump card when you don't have to?'

Sarah thought a moment, musing over the wisdom of his remark, then said: 'Both of you ride with me. And if either of you get so much as an inkling that he's stalling me or knows more than he's telling, tug on your ear. I'll do the rest.'

Sheriff Forbes lived in a small green-and-white clapboard house on a dirt hillside overlooking the rooftops lining Main Street. It was set back from the road leading up to it and alongside it was a corral containing the sheriff's sorrel. The house was dark and after making sure there were no rear windows or doors, we dismounted and Sarah pounded on the front door.

She had to pound again, harder, before someone stirred inside. Then a lamp flared and I could hear the sheriff cussing as he plodded to the door.

'Yeah, yeah, yeah, who is it?'

'Sarah Eckers, Sheriff.'

'Who?'

'Sarah Eckers. I work for the railroad. We need to talk.'

'Come to my office in the mornin'.'

'By then it might be too late.'

The sheriff cussed again. Then the door opened and the lumpy, towering shape of Lonnie Forbes appeared. In faded red long johns that were tucked into scuffed cowboy boots, he held a hurricane lamp in one fist, a Colt .45 in the other.

'Goddammit,' he grumbled, 'what the hell do you' — he frowned as he saw Cassidy and me — 'three want at this hour?'

As Sarah showed the sheriff her ID and briefly explained what we'd heard, Cassidy and I watched his face, his eyes especially, to see his reaction. I'm no mind reader so I can't say exactly what he was thinking, and from Cassidy's shrug I guessed he couldn't either. But my gut feeling was that Forbes was genuinely surprised by the idea of the Colbert brothers pulling a hold-up in Santa Rosa.

'Come on in,' he said as Sarah finished. 'I'll throw on some clothes and maybe we can figure out the Colberts' plan . . . and how to stop 'em.'

There was a pot of cold, left-over coffee on the stove. As the sheriff got dressed, I stoked the coals under it while Cassidy lit another lamp and set it on the table. The coffee was hot and strong enough to wake a corpse by the time the four of us sat down to talk.

'Well, there're no cattle buyers in town,' Sheriff Forbes said, 'so it don't make sense to hold up the bank — '

'Then it has to be the train,' Sarah said. 'Probably the early one from El Paso.'

'That don't make sense neither,' the sheriff said. 'It's a freight.'

'That doesn't mean there isn't an express car,' Sarah said. 'And if there is it could be carrying gold or silver bullion.'

'Even if you're right, why hold it up here?' put in Cassidy. 'There's plenty of open track 'tween here and El Paso and no lawmen for miles around.'

'You're forgetting somethin',' I said. ''Cording to that barkeep in El Tecalote, the Colberts only left Palomas an hour or two 'fore we did. They wouldn't have had time to ride that far.'

''Sides it ain't easy to stop a freight goin' full bore,' the sheriff said.

'Why even try,' said Sarah, 'when it stops here to take on water? About what time would that be, Lonnie?'

'Eight-oh-six,' the sheriff said, 'if it's on time.'

'Is it usually on time?' I asked.

'Give or take a few minutes, yeah.'

'Then you got time to deputize some men,' Cassidy said softly.

Sheriff Forbes grunted. 'Time ain't the problem, Luke. It's findin' men with the guts to face the Colbert gang if it comes to a showdown.'

'Can't say as I blame them,' Sarah said. 'If I had a family, and knew how vicious the Colbert brothers are, I'm not sure if I'd volunteer either.'

'Surprise is on our side,' I reminded. 'With three or four extra guns we could most likely get the jump on them an' there wouldn't even be no shootin'.'

Sheriff Forbes finished his coffee, got to his feet and buckled on his gunbelt. 'Reckon I know at least three men I can count on, men who won't be afraid of retribution. After that it'll be pot luck.'

Sarah rose and looked out the window. The sky in the east was still muddy but now a faint tinge of yellow showed beyond the mountains.

'Then we'd better get riding,' she said. 'It'll be dawn in less than an hour,'

27

Dawn had come, flooding the muddy-gray sky with streaks of lavender, green and gold as we dismounted in front of Gustafson's Livery Stable. Lars had been one of the men we'd aroused, and though he was willing to fight beside us the sheriff wouldn't hear of it.

'You just make sure our horses stay hid, old timer,' he told the Swede. 'If the Colberts see 'em tied up outside the station, they might figure somethin' is up and ride off 'fore we can brace them.'

'I do as you ask,' Lars agreed. 'T''is promise I make.'

'It would also help if you'd try and keep everyone away from the station,' Sarah said, 'so they can't get hurt by any stray bullets.'

Lars nodded. 'This I also promise.'

'Fair enough,' Sheriff Forbes said.

'Then unless someone's got a question, let's get started.'

We all made sure our weapons were fully loaded then headed for the railroad. It wasn't much of a walk. Even so I kept close to Sarah to make sure she didn't grow weak or start bleeding again.

Lee Hargrove, the telegraph operator, came with us. A small rabbit-faced man with a greasy comb-over, he refused to fight but willingly telegraphed the railroad office in El Paso to see if the train was on time. A reply came almost immediately: it would be seven minutes late.

'Ask the operator if he knows whether there's a gold shipment on board,' Sheriff Forbes told Hargrove.

'I doubt if he'd tell us even if he did know,' said Sarah.

'He might,' Hargrove replied. 'He's my cousin.'

'Go ahead,' the sheriff urged. 'It's worth a try.'

But Hargrove's cousin, Holcomb,

replied that he had no knowledge of any gold or silver shipment. What's more, he added, he hadn't seen any armed guards on board the train when it left El Paso — only boxcars carrying soldiers that he figured were going home on furlough.

'Reckon you dragged us out of bed for nothin', Sheriff,' grumbled Luther Folkes, one of the three men who'd agreed to fight with us.

The other two — Miles Hubbell and Ruben Wykopff — looked equally sour.

'Don't blame Lonnie,' Sarah told them. 'I'm the one who said the Colbert gang might be riding this way. You fellas got any gripes, direct them at me.'

'Fat lot of good that'll do us,' Wykopff grumbled.

'Yeah,' echoed Hubbell. 'When the rest of the town hears 'bout this, we'll all be laughing stocks!'

'Tell you what,' Sheriff Forbes said. 'If nothin' comes of this, you can all have a steak breakfast on me. Fair enough?'

Nodding, the three men grudgingly subsided.

'Thing I can't figure out,' said Cassidy, 'is, if the train ain't carryin' gold or silver, then what the hell are the Colberts after?'

Before anyone could answer, it hit me. 'Guns!' I blurted.

Everyone turned to me.

'What about them?' Sarah said.

'The Colberts aren't after gold or silver — it's guns!'

'Guns?'

Everyone frowned, puzzled.

'What guns?'

'Government-issue carbines. Most likely a whole shipment of them along with *mucho* ammo to boot.'

'What in tarnation makes you say that?' demanded Sheriff Forbes.

''Cause it all adds up,' I said. Then to Hargrove: 'Those soldiers your cousin saw on the train — they weren't on furlough, they're guardin' the guns.'

Silence.

Everyone exchanged looks.

189

I could tell they weren't sold on the idea but at the same time, none of them disagreed.

'Maybe I'm thick-headed,' the sheriff said. 'But I still don't get it — '

'No, no, it makes sense,' Cassidy interrupted. 'One night a while back, when I was in the Acme Saloon in El Paso, I heard some cavalrymen talkin' about how the army plans to build a fort 'tween here and Lordsburg. You know. So they can protect the settlers and miners from renegade Apaches. They'd need guns for that.'

Again, no one disagreed.

'Let's hope carbines are all they're shipping,' Sarah muttered.

'Meaning?' I said.

'If Luke's right and the army is planning on setting up a fort, chances are they'll also ship a cannon or two and . . . maybe even a Gatling gun.'

Everyone froze.

'Jesus,' I muttered. 'Can you imagine what the Colbert brothers would do with a Gatling gun?'

'I don't want to,' Sarah said grimly.

No one else did either.

'Be like giving 'em a license to kill,' Luther Folkes said.

Sheriff Forbes sighed, spat his disgust in the dirt and tongued his Redman chew to the other cheek. 'All right, calm down, everyone. Let's not throw a shoe. A Gatling gun ups the ante, that's for sure, but it don't change what we're here for — and that's to stop the Colberts from gettin' their hands on those carbines.'

'Just how do you plan on doin' that?' Cassidy asked.

Sheriff Forbes spat in the dirt again. 'Keep it simple, I always say. When the gang rides up, we let 'em get off their horses and then close in.'

'Get the drop on 'em?'

The sheriff nodded.

'And if they won't give up without a fight?' Hubbell said. 'What then?'

'We gun 'em down.'

''Mean in cold blood?' Wykopff questioned.

Cassidy spoke before the sheriff could. 'Damn right,' he said softly. 'This here's a gunfight, gents, not tiddly-winks.'

'I never killed nobody in cold blood,' Folkes said. 'Truth is, I ain't killed nobody at all. Ever.'

'Me neither,' Hubbell admitted.

'I shot them two drifters who tried to rob my store last year,' Wykopff said. 'Neither of 'em died, but I pulled the trigger. That ought to count for something.'

''Course it counts,' Sheriff Forbes said. 'Wasn't your fault the Good Lord chose to let the bastards live.' He included the rest of us as he added: 'Now, is everyone clear on what we're goin' to do?'

We all nodded.

Hargrove licked his lips uneasily. 'If you're done with me, Sheriff, reckon I'll be headin' home.'

'Go ahead. But don't tell nobody what's goin' on here. I don't want word leakin' out. Might reach the ears of some relative or friend of the Colberts an' next thing you know, we're the ones walkin' into a trap.'

'Speaking of traps,' I said, as Hargrove hurried off, 'where do you want us to hide?'

'Split up and find cover beside the tracks from here to the water-tower. An' nobody start firin' till I give the signal.'

'Where will you be?' Sarah enquired.

'Inside,' he said, thumbing at the station-house. 'At the window.'

'What's the signal?' Cassidy asked quietly.

'All of you keep your eye on me,' Sheriff Forbes said. 'Soon as the Colberts get off their horses, I'm goin' to order 'em to throw down their guns — '

'An' if they refuse?' I said.

'Shoot to kill.'

28

Sarah and I took cover behind some rocks near the station-house. We were only a few paces apart and could easily see each other in the misty, yellowing dawn light. I was still worried about her condition, but when I asked her how she was feeling, she smiled bravely and said: 'Fine.'

I knew she was anything but fine. But I also knew there wasn't anything I could do or say that would make her give up this chance to finally put an end to the Colbert brothers and their gang.

Dawn turned into early misty morning . . . with still no sign of the Colbert gang.

I could hear the others talking to one another in hissed whispers.

I looked at Sarah and she held up ten fingers.

I nodded to show I understood,

thinking: *Only ten minutes before the train arrives and still no sign of the Colberts. Hell, maybe the gang isn't planning to steal the guns after all.*

It was wishful thinking. Because at that moment I — and probably everyone else — heard horses approaching. They were still some distance away. But by the faint, rhythmic sound of thudding hoofs everybody knew the riders were coming from the border and we all looked in that direction.

'Remember,' the sheriff called out from the station-house window, 'nobody pulls a trigger till I do.'

I glanced at Sarah. She wasn't expecting me to look her way and I caught her off-guard. She was leaned over her rifle, supporting herself on it, obviously in great pain. Keeping ducked down, I hurried to her side.

She heard me coming and quickly straightened up. 'W-What're you doing?' she whispered. 'Why'd you come over here?'

Ignoring her questions, I leaned my

Winchester against the rocks and gently pulled her around so that she faced me. Instantly I saw the blood reddening her shirt. I started to unbutton it but she angrily knocked my hand away, saying: 'Don't!'

'Dammit, Sarah, you're bleeding!'

'Get back to your position,' she snapped.

'Save your breath,' I said firmly. 'I'm stayin'.'

'Damn you, Macahan! This isn't about us. Can't you see that?'

'I can see you're bleeding, Sarah. That's all I care about.'

'In that case you needn't worry. One of the stitches pulled apart, is all. Just some minor bleeding and . . . and . . .'
She let go of her rifle, swayed unsteadily and would have fallen if I hadn't grabbed her.

Leaning her back against the rocks, I gently unbuttoned her shirt and peeled the wet side back from her shoulder. Even in the misty morning-light I could see blood seeping from her reopened wound. I quickly unknotted my necker-chief, wadded it up and pressed it against the wound.

'Hold that in place,' I told her. 'Don't argue,' I exclaimed as she started to protest. 'Just do as I say!'

Grudgingly she obeyed me. As gently as I could, I cut off the sleeve of her shirt. She winced but didn't make a sound. I wrapped the sleeve over her shoulder and under her arm and knotted it, holding my neckerchief in position. Then I rebuttoned her shirt.

Meanwhile, the sound of approach-ing horses was getting closer. I glanced toward the border. My heart jumped. Riding toward us, shrouded by mist, were more than a dozen outlaws.

Sarah saw them too. She gave me a quick, grateful look then pulled her six-shooter from its holster.

'Here,' I said, placing my Colt on the rock beside her. 'Use mine as well, an' give a holler when you need to reload.'

'What about you?'

I answered by grabbing my rifle, and

hers, and turned to face the oncoming riders.

They were now close enough to see their grim, mist-shrouded faces. The Colbert brothers were in the lead, followed by the rest of the gang. I'm not one to duck a fight or any other kind of trouble, but at that moment I felt a tingling sense of apprehension, and wondered if my time had come. As for the others, especially the barkeep and the store-owners who'd agreed to fight with us, I could only guess how scared they must have been right now.

I wanted to give their courage a boost by shooting one of the outlaws. But I wasn't running the show, and stifling my frustration I rested my Winchester on a rock and took careful aim at the lead rider, Judd Colbert.

Having no idea he was only a trigger-squeeze from death, he led the gang to the railroad tracks and there abruptly reined up, his horse coming to a sliding stop. The others behind him did the same. The damp mist kept the dust from rising and I could see the outlaws looking suspiciously around for any signs of trouble.

The moments crawled by. Even in the cool morning air my palms grew damp. But the Colbert gang was too experienced to rush things. They continued to sit astride their restless horses, hands on their guns, heads swiveling, squinting as they strained to see in the swirling white mist.

Finally Judd, satisfied that no danger awaited them, nudged his horse forward and motioned for the others to follow him. The gang rode on across the tracks and reined up in front of the station-house. I could hear their voices, muffled by the mist, but couldn't make out what they were saying.

I glanced at Sarah. She was glaring fixedly at the Colberts, her dark-green eyes smoldering with anger, six-gun trained on the brothers as they dismounted and looped their reins over the tie-rail.

One of the outlaws turned to Judd.

'How much time we got afore — ?'

Sheriff Forbes cut him off. 'All of you,' he barked, poking his rifle out the station-house window, 'grab the air!'

29

The startled outlaws froze for an instant.

'You heard me,' the sheriff snapped. 'Get them hands up. Now!'

Some of the outlaws hesitantly obeyed.

Not the Colberts. All three brothers grabbed for their guns and spun around to face the window.

Sheriff Forbes surprised me. Huge and lumbering as he was, I hadn't figured him for a man of action. But he got off two shots, so fast they sounded like one, and Judd Colbert staggered back, legs buckling, and fell to his knees. He remained there for a moment with a shocked almost bewildered expression, as if unable to believe he was hit, and then pitched forward onto his face, dead.

Meanwhile, all hell had erupted.

Even as Judd was shot his brothers, Sloane and Laird, and the rest of the gang opened fire at the sheriff. Their bullets splintered the window frame and shattered the upper glass, causing shards to fly everywhere.

None hit the sheriff, who'd ducked back inside, and before the outlaws could rush the station-house Sarah and I started firing at them.

Cassidy and the others immediately joined in.

Too late, the surprised gang realized they were caught in a crossfire. Two went down almost immediately and didn't get up. A third man was also hit but managed to stay on his feet and fired at me. He missed but his bullets ricocheted off the rocks about my head, forcing me to duck down.

The rest of the gang, led by the Colberts, ran for the nearest cover and desperately returned fire.

Beside me, Sarah kept firing until she ran out of bullets and then stubbornly tried to reload her guns. Her injured shoulder made any movement with her left arm painfully difficult and she winced. I quickly crawled to her, reloaded both Colts and gave them to her. She smiled her thanks, though her gritted expression made it clear that she hated having to need my help. She could only shoot with her right hand, which meant firing one gun at a time, but she was so damned accurate I swear it didn't matter.

Staying close, so I could again reload for her, I peered over the rock in front of me. It was an experience I'll always remember. Everyone still alive seemed to be shooting at once. The booming gunfire was thunderous. Ricocheting bullets whined everywhere. I've heard old gunfighters and Civil War veterans brag about shootouts and battles they were in where the air was filled with flying lead. I never believed them. Till now.

It was worse than sticking your head into a swarm of angry wasps.

Taking a chance, I rested my rifle on

the rock protecting me and snapped off a shot at Laird Colbert, who was crouched behind the station-house. My bullet splintered the wood beside his face. He jerked back, cussing, and ran toward a row of rocks. I fired at him, but missed, and before I could lever in another round he dived behind the rocks.

Shifting my aim, I fired twice at Mel Casper, one of the outlaws Sarah and I'd seen in Palomas. On one knee, he was peering around the rear of an abandoned buckboard that sat rotting in the sun on the other side of the tracks; my bullet hit one of the rusted wheels, glanced off and punched a hole through his Adam's apple. He made a gurgling sound, dropped his rifle and slumped against the wheel, blood pumping from his throat.

But elsewhere things weren't going well for us. Though five outlaws lay dead, there was still more than twice our number alive and once they were safely behind cover, they began shooting with deadly accuracy.

Hubbell died first. I heard him gasp and saw him stagger out from behind a rocky outcrop. He was bleeding from the mouth and blood streamed from a gaping wound above his temple. After a few stumbling steps, he collapsed face-down on the ground . . . and didn't move again.

Incensed that a mild-mannered, decent storekeeper like Hubbell should die from a renegade's bullet, I pumped round after round into a clump of ocotillo bushes growing on the far side of the tracks. I'd seen two outlaws dive behind them earlier . . . and now had the satisfaction of hearing cries of pain. Silence followed. I wasn't sure if I'd killed either man, but knew I'd definitely wounded them — maybe fatally — as from then on there was no more shooting.

Moments later the barkeep, Wykopff, was hit. He'd been lying on the bank of a dry river-bed across the tracks and on hearing him yelp, I peered around the rocks to see if I could tell how badly he was hurt. But he was already writhing on the ground and before I could run to his side, bullets chipped away pieces of rock near my head and I was forced to duck down.

'Wykopff's caught one,' I told Sarah.

She stopped shooting and nodded. 'In the chest. I saw him drop.'

'Damn,' I said. 'We're runnin' out of warm bodies.'

'And ammo.' She pointed to her gunbelt, which held only a few cartridges and then went on shooting.

'Be sure to save the last one for yourself.'

'Don't worry,' she replied. 'I've no intention of being a plaything for the Colberts or when they've used me up, being sold in Mexico. Here,' she added, handing me my Colt, 'I'm out again.'

I didn't have many cartridges left myself and once they were gone . . .

For the first time it hit me that I might actually die, right here and now. As the reality sank in I realized it didn't bother me as much as I'd expected it would. Surprised, and figuring that it had to do with the way I'd been wasting my life, I started to reload the Peacemaker. As I did, there was a momentary lull in the shooting and I thought I heard something familiar in the distance.

'You hear that?' I asked Sarah.

'What?'

'Listen.'

She listened then looked relieved. 'Train's coming.'

As she spoke I heard the whistle again, closer now, louder, and grinned. 'Looks like those soldier boys are goin' to earn their wages.'

''Least now they won't walk into an ambush,' she said grimly. She went on shooting with her own gun. Her accuracy was uncanny. First, one of the Colbert's cousins dropped. Moments later an outlaw I didn't recognize collapsed with a bullet in his brain. Sarah then turned her attention to Sloane, her steady shooting keeping him pinned down behind the same rocks that also hid his brother. 'What's more,' she added as she reloaded, 'if the cavalry get here soon enough to swing the fight in our favor, we'll put an end to the Colbert gang once and for all.'

It was an agreeable thought. I looked eastward along the glinting tracks. The sun was burning off the mist and I could now see black smoke spiraling up in the distance and knew the train would soon be here.

Just then Laird poked his head above the rocks. I fired several rounds at him. He ducked down. I kept firing, the ricocheting bullets chasing him from behind one rock to another, until I finally ran out of ammo.

Sarah, who'd been watching the train, said impatiently: 'C'mon, c'mon . . .'

'Let's just hope it stops,' I said as I reloaded.

'Why the devil wouldn't it?'

'No reason.'

'Don't lie to me, dammit. What

makes you think the train mightn't stop?'

'Well, it just occurred to me: if the engineer hears the shootin' or somehow gets wind of what's goin' on, he might just barrel on through and take on water from somewhere down the line.'

'Christ,' she said glumly.

'Don't worry,' I assured her. 'It'll stop. It's got to . . . '

The outlaws must have seen the train coming too — and came to the same conclusion. Because at the angry urging of the Colbert brothers, the gang blasted away at us.

'Stay down!' I barked, as bullets zipped about our heads. 'They're tryin' to end this quickly.'

Sarah didn't respond. I turned and looked at her. She sat slumped against the rocks, eyes closed, lips a tight white line, one hand clutching her injured shoulder.

At first I thought she was just in pain. Then I noticed that her fingers were glistening. Alarmed, I leaned close and realized that her shirt was soaked through with fresh blood.

'Sarah . . . Sarah, for Chris'sake . . . you OK?'

She opened her eyes and smiled weakly. 'Fine.'

But she wasn't. Her eyelids fluttered weakly then closed, and her head lolled to one side.

I put my ear to her chest but couldn't hear her heart beating. I felt sick to my gut. She wasn't the first woman I'd seen die; but she was the first woman, other than my mother, to die that I'd ever respected or cared about.

There was a dull roaring in my ears that drowned out the shooting.

And hid the train whistle, too.

Inside, all I could feel was white-hot rage.

I don't remember taking back my Colt. I don't remember reloading it. Hell, I don't even remember getting up.

What I do remember is finding myself walking toward the rocks that hid the Colbert brothers, teeth gritted, hand resting on the butt of my six-shooter, all sense of reason and compassion replaced by a desire for vengeance.

Meanwhile, in the background all I could make out were vague, blurred images . . . glimpses of the train approaching, smoke belching from its stack, the gleaming black engine closer now . . . with blue-coated soldiers riding inside and on top of the boxcars . . . while others stood on flatbed cars . . . rifles at the ready . . . a Gatling gun mounted on a tripod tied down behind them.

. . . And closer, near the station-house, the remaining outlaws, led by Laird and Sloane Colbert, running for their horses.

. . . And closer still, the tall lean figure of Luke Cassidy, Schofield holstered on his right hip, striding purposefully toward the outlaws.

. . . And behind him, in silhouette, Sheriff Forbes firing out the window of the station-house, picking them off before they could get mounted.

30

I quickly caught up to Cassidy and matched him stride-for-stride.

If he saw me, he didn't show it. He just stared straight ahead, jut-jawed and silent.

Together, we grimly strode toward the outlaws. Not one of them noticed us. By now they had untied their horses and the animals, panicked by the shooting and approaching train, were rearing and fighting to break loose, making it difficult for the gunmen to mount them.

Even more alarming for the outlaws, the train was now almost at the station and the soldiers were getting ready to jump off and join in the fight.

Suddenly escape was impossible.

That's when the two Colbert brothers, Laird and Sloane, turned toward Cassidy and me. Knowing how gutless they were, I expected them to throw down their six-shooters and raise their hands in surrender.

But I hadn't counted on something: how the thought of dangling from a rope can force a man — even a gutless man — to stand and fight.

Trapped and desperate, Laird and Sloane jerked their guns.

It was a fatal mistake.

Cassidy and I drew and fired almost simultaneously.

Laird and Sloane staggered back, six-shooters dropping from their limp fingers, each with a bullet in his heart, both dead as they slumped to the ground.

Blood racing, I turned to Cassidy who was holstering his Schofield.

'How's the woman?' he demanded.

I shook my head.

'Damn,' he murmured. 'That stinks.' He looked at the dead Colbert brothers, adding: 'You know, *amigo*, I planned on shooting 'em in the gut so they'd die slowly — like my brother.

213

But force of habit . . . ' He shook his head in disgust. 'I'll go to my grave hatin' myself for this.' Before I could say anything, he turned and walked off.

Meanwhile, the train had pulled into the station and soldiers were piling off, rifles trained on the remaining outlaws. The death of the Colberts had punched all the fight out of them. As one, they grabbed air and surrendered.

Sheriff Forbes emerged from the station-house. On his way to me, he passed Cassidy. He spoke to him but Cassidy ignored the big lawman and kept on walking toward town.

The sheriff looked after him for a moment, puzzled, and then joined me. 'What the deuce is eating him?'

'It's a long story,' I said, adding bitterly, 'and before you wonder what's eating me, there's a good woman lying back there and I'm goin' to miss her more than I care to admit.'

The sheriff frowned. 'Eckers is dead?'

I nodded.

'Damn. I surely hate to hear that.

Much as I'm against women bein' lawmen, she was good enough to make me eat my words.'

He sounded sincere but I was in no mood to be charitable. 'I'm taking her body back to town an' then notifyin' the railroad,' I said. 'I want to make sure Sarah gets buried the way she deserves.'

'Let me know how that goes, son. If they ain't willing to do what's right, I'll talk to the mayor — see if he's agreeable to Santa Rosa footin' the bill.'

'Thanks, I appreciate that.'

'It's the least I can do. Wait,' he added as I started away, 'hold up, Ezra . . . '

It was the first time he'd ever called me by my first name. Surprised, I looked back at him, my tone more charitable as I said: 'Yeah?'

'Know what else you should do?'

'Tell me.'

'Think about fillin' her shoes.'

I almost laughed. 'Be a railroad dick?'

'That or some other kind of lawman.'

'A marshal or a sheriff like you, maybe?'

'There's worse ways to earn a dollar.'

'Can't think of one.'

'Go ahead. Sass me. But before you start spittin' on my star, Macahan, there's somethin' you ought to keep in mind: not every man's got the steel for it. You do. I've watched you. You got nerve when it counts . . . and it'd be a damn shame if you didn't put it to good use.' He turned away before I could respond.

I watched as he walked toward the soldiers, who had now rounded up the outlaws and were awaiting orders from two officers talking nearby.

Lawman? I asked myself.

Sheriff Ezra Macahan?

Deputy US Marshal Macahan?

Marshal Macahan?

Strangely, it didn't sound as absurd as I'd expected.

In fact, it had a nice ring to it.

And as I sadly made my way back to Sarah, who was now being examined by an army medic, I wondered if fate, with its strange twisted logic, had sent her my way for that very reason — to give purpose to a young man's life that up till now had been pretty much a pure waste of time.

On reaching Sarah, I started to tell the doctor that I was taking her body into town, but he waved me silent. Then, stuffing his stethoscope into the pocket of his tunic, he straightened up and said: 'Stay with her till I get my bag!'

'But, Doc — '

'That's an order!' he barked. He hurried off toward the train.

Puzzled, I knelt beside Sarah and sadly cradled her head against me.

'Damn you to hell,' I whispered to her. 'Why'd you have to go an' die on me?'

I bent and kissed her on the forehead.

That's when she opened her eyes and weakly smiled at me.

SCATTERGUN SMITH

Max Gunn

When Scattergun Smith sets out after the infamous outlaw Bradley Black, his search leads him across dangerous terrain, and every fibre of his being tells him that he is travelling headfirst into the jaws of trouble. But Black has both wronged the youngster Smith and killed innocent people, and has to pay. Scattergun is determined to catch and end the life of the ruthless outlaw before Black claims fresh victims. It will take every ounce of his renowned expertise to stop him, and prove why he is called Scattergun Smith.

A FINAL SHOOT-OUT

J. D. Kincaid

When Abe Fletcher is released from prison, he's anxious to reclaim his inheritance — a beautiful and flourishing ranch. At the same time, bank robbers Red Ned Davis and Hank Jolley are fleeing from justice and holed up with Jolley's cousin, Vic Morgan. After a chance encounter between Abe and Vic, the outlaws agree to help Abe regain his inheritance — for a price. However, their plans go awry due to the unexpected intervention of a seductive saloon singer, Arizona Audrey, and the famous Kentuckian gunfighter, Jack Stone . . .